Readers are saying:

"If you are looking for a schmexy quick read without a lot of angst, grab this book!"

— Becky M.

"The chemistry between the characters kept me totally hooked until the very last page!"

— Kathleen B.

"Well-written hidden gem... I love the openly awkward nature of the characters. It was wildly refreshing and realistic."

— Terrisha B.

"The description of their first sexual encounter was amazingly told, steamy, hot."

— Judith

"Relatable characters who have a tension that will keep you riveted. Definitely recommend for the mature reader who likes some heat!"

— Rachel W.-M.

Summer Seduction

Aria Glazki

Anika Press

*For those staying
steadfastly true to themselves*

Chapter One

TARALYNN HARWOOD BREATHED a sigh of relief as she stepped out of the stuffy event room. After an intensive Q&A and signing almost fifty autographs, the cool quiet of the hotel lobby was like finding freedom. As much as she loved her fans, engaging with an endless stream of strangers was still, in a word, exhausting. Thank goodness for Lani, her kickass assistant who'd handle all the wrap-up from the signing. Which meant Taralynn could grab a well-deserved cocktail.

The strappy stilettos she wore to every signing clacked on the polished lobby floor as she strode over to the dimly lit hotel lounge. By the time the bartender slid her pear martini onto the reflective black bar, Tracy had almost entirely shed the constrictive second skin of her alter ego. If you didn't count the glammed-up outfit, that was.

She pulled out her phone to check any missed notifications, skimming through tagged photos from the signing—already up online—as she lifted the chilled glass to her lips. The martini was the perfect balm after hours spent socializing. Taralynn might be all about the bawdy jokes, double entendres, and candid conversations about kink, but Tracy preferred the invisibility of sitting in a quiet bar. Splurging on a delicious drink after a book signing had become her little tradition, ever since there'd been no one to celebrate with after her first one. One of the trade-offs of being an erotic romance author.

Tracy re-shared a particularly fun shot of Taralynn with a group of readers who'd come decked out in some—fairly mild—BDSM accoutrements, then turned her phone over. She leaned back on the bar stool and sipped the perfectly balanced drink, her eyes shutting in pleasure as the hint of pear washed over her taste buds. Sometimes, it really was the little things.

"You make that look," said a male voice to her left, "like the most amazing drink ever."

And just like that, Taralynn was back. Yes, she had male readers, too, which meant tonight everyone was only meeting Taralynn, just in case. She swallowed nonchalantly, opened her eyes, and lowered the martini glass to the bar, all while curving her lips up in a sultry smile. "Let's just say it hit the spot."

The man who'd spoken sat a couple barstools away, the collar to his button-down shirt flipped open above a loosened tie. So maybe he was at the hotel for a business thing, not her "Tantalized by Taralynn" event. He was cute, if nondescript, at least in the muted lighting. Brown hair, just long enough to run fingers through, clean-shaven, eyes of an uncertain color, a flawlessly straight nose. Forgettable, if not for the slightly pro-truding ears, the lovely cushions of his lips, and the intense—almost predatory—gaze.

"I'd love to buy you another," he said, fingers fanning to-ward her drink.

"A bit premature, don't you think?"

His eyes dipped to her lips then lower, to her artificially pushed-up bust, before meeting her gaze again. "God forbid," he said, a new hoarseness underlying his voice. Was that a blush caressing his cheeks, or a trick of the lighting?

He shifted in his seat, revealing a tumbler with the remnants of a dark drink that he promptly drained. "I've, uh." He cut himself off, shaking his head at the now empty glass before setting it aside. "I've read almost all your books. Those I could find."

Ah. That sounded like her cue to finish her drink, sign another book—or napkin, or whatever—and head home. "Then I certainly hope you enjoyed them."

"They were…quite informative."

Tracy hummed, taking another sip rather than comment. She was supposed to be done with work for the night, not entertaining another fan for a private Q&A. Or worse, providing fodder for his later fantasies. Some people were incapable of separating the author from the sex in her books.

"I was sorry to have missed your talk, I got caught up at work," he offered, his lips slanting in a smirk. He shook his head again, like he was in the middle of calling himself an idiot. "Anyway, I'll leave you to your evening." He turned away, signaling the bartender for another drink.

The pressure of being "on" popped, letting that sense of freedom trickle back in. Her unnamed companion rolled his empty tumbler between his palms. "What is it you do?" Tracy found herself asking.

"Oh, it's pretty boring," he said down to the bar, then stiffened. His head swiveled to look back up at her. "I work for a marketing firm, analyzing the effectiveness of keywords and other campaign analytics so I can recommend adjustments." He smiled in that slightly sad, self-deprecating way. "Sounds thrilling, right?"

"Sounds baffling," Tracy said honestly. As an author, all that cost-per-click and keyword stuff was supposed to be part of the deal, but she'd never been able to wrap her mind around it. Another thing Lani took care of for her, now that Tracy could afford an assistant.

The man tilted his new drink in her direction, then stalled, zeroing in on her glass. "Refill?" he asked, one eyebrow quirking up.

Tracy followed his gaze to the waiting last sip. On the one hand, going home, getting out of her sexy/professional outfit, and curling up with something simple like mac and cheese sounded just about perfect, especially since her wide belt was digging into her ribcage. On the other, how long had it been since she'd even been on a date? Having a drink with a decent-looking man who seemed nice and harmless enough wasn't the worst fate in the world. Plus, it would save her the hassle of dressing up separately for a date, if she ever did go back on one of the neglected dating apps downloaded to her phone.

And here she was, sitting next to someone at least a little interesting, if only because he didn't mind admitting he read *those* books.

Still… "I tend not to drink with someone before I even know their name."

His smile became a little more genuine, if still as crooked. But now it was endearing rather than tainted by a touch of bitterness. "Jeremy." He signaled again to the bartender, then shifted to the barstool beside Tracy. Closer, a hint of stubble was visible on his jaw, and those intense eyes turned out to be on the greener side of hazel. She could certainly do worse. And maybe they could have some fun.

Anticipation zinged through Jeremy as he leaned against the wall outside the door to Taralynn's apartment. He'd expected her to blow him off, not even give him a second glance beyond the same polite attention she'd paid everyone who came up for an autograph. He'd told her he missed the event, but really he'd only missed the formal Q&A. He'd snuck in, watching awhile as the line of fans shuffled toward the plastic table piled with books. And if he wasn't mistaken, custom-printed pasties.

Like a moron, he'd been too intimidated to wait his turn, go up and meet the woman who'd helped pick up the pieces when his life fell apart. When she'd sat down near him at the bar… Well, the last thing he'd expected was to be going home with her. If she ever let him in, that was.

After he'd kissed her out in the hotel lobby, she'd warned him: she had conditions. But hell, given everything she described in her books, of course being with her would be an adventure. Her books were so hot, and so useful, Jeremy was up for trying just about anything with her.

The door swung open silently and she stepped out, holding up a folded sheet of paper and a pen. Meeting the challenge in her eyes, Jeremy flipped open the paper. NON-DISCLOSURE AGREEMENT was printed across the top, with a handful of bullets beneath it.

He glanced back to Taralynn, catching a softer expression, a vulnerability that matched the sporadic glimpses he'd gotten of something other than her salacious public persona. But he wasn't one to kiss and tell, anyway. And what man in his right mind would turn down a night with Taralynn Harwood?

Jeremy took the pen from her fingers, flattened the sheet on the wall, and signed somewhere near the line on the bottom of the page.

"Date," she said when he offered the NDA back to her. She had taken the time inside her apartment to put a fresh coat of color on her lips, too. They shone a dark red in the yellow of the hallway light.

Jeremy squinted at the sheet, found the shorter line, and added the date. He skimmed the legalese, but damned if his dick wasn't the one making all the decisions now. If whatever they were about to do required an NDA, it was bound to be one hell of a night.

Chapter Two

TRACY ARCHED INTO THE KISS, running her palms down Jeremy's bare torso. His mouth demanded more, lips and tongue dominating as if he wanted to devour her. Her hands slipped to the zipper of his slacks, his other clothes already discarded somewhere in her living room, along with most of hers.

He grunted as her fingers undid the zipper. The pants slid to the floor, his belt buckle thumping against her rug, and he kicked the material aside. Calloused hands that belied his office job gripped her waist, lifting her off her toes. Her legs curled around his thighs. The kiss eased as he stepped them to her bed, the gentle sliding of lips filling her breasts with the heaviness of desire.

Those lips broke away to tease her neck as his weight settled above her on the bed. Tracy gripped the silken strength of his biceps, running one foot along his leg as her lungs filled with the cool, fresh air. Jeremy found a particularly sensitive spot near her collar and she shivered, bumping gently against him.

His hand fumbled under her back until the binding pressure of her bra popped loose. She gasped, and his teeth grazed her neck before he laved the spot with his tongue. He sat back to lift away her bra, pressing his hips intimately against her. Her fingers traced over the ridges of his surprisingly defined abs. His eyes darkened as he took in the freed mounds of her breasts, thumbs brushing over her nipples. She pulled him closer, displacing his hands and bending to taste the spot below his ear. His stubble prickled against her cheek.

He shifted away, trailing hot kisses over her sternum, down her stomach. One hand cupped her breast, molding it with faint pressure, careful to avoid the straining peak. He bit near her belly button, and his thumb finally brushed oh-so-lightly over her nipple, drawing a guttural moan from her throat as her fingers dug into his hair.

The teasing contrast continued, the pull of his nibbles up her abdomen matched with soft flicks of his fingers. Hadn't she written something like this once?

His mouth found her neglected other breast, moist heat closing over that nipple as his fingers pinched the other. Tracy's breath came in unsteady gasps, her fingers splaying on his back as he continued the deliberate torture—then switched sides. The friction of his hips occasionally bumping against her no longer seemed accidental, either.

His palm slid from her breast, down her stomach, but then over her hip as she wriggled involuntarily against him. His mouth lifted to her lips, pressing them open in a domineering kiss before breaking away to land back at her bellybutton. His fingers curled under the band of her fairly practical boy shorts, tongue swirling languidly down her belly.

Oh, no. Tracy's hands found his, gripping to keep them—and her underwear—in place. Bringing a guy home hadn't been anywhere on her radar for tonight. What if he expected nothing but a landing strip—or a full-on Brazilian—instead of her somewhat trimmed but mostly natural state?

Worse, what if she just didn't *taste* good?

"Wait," she managed to gasp out.

Jeremy looked up, resting his chin on the fabric of her panties. Moments ago, she would have squirmed at the intimate pressure. Now, mortification had taken over, freezing her in place.

"Stop," she said, her voice a bit more steady.

"Just tell me what you like." He dropped a kiss just above where his chin had been resting. "I'm willing to learn," he added against the sensitive skin, the words vibrating through her.

Tracy clung to the foolproof phrase that had extricated her before. "I don't want to do this." She let go of his hands to cross an arm over her chest.

Jeremy's mouth popped open. He shook his head, eyebrows dipping down in his confusion. And then he sat up. He hesitated, waiting for her to change her mind or maybe trying to figure out a way to change it for her. But eventually he said, "Okay."

"You should go," Tracy said, scooting up the bed, away from him.

He nodded, scooped up his pants, and left, letting the bedroom door drift closed behind him.

Tracy shut her eyes, blowing out one long breath, then burrowed under her comforter. If only it could offer the kind of comfort she needed.

✧ ✧ ✧

Damn it. Jeremy patted his pockets one more time as he scanned the floor. But there was really only one place his wallet could have fallen: in Taralynn's bedroom.

What the hell had happened? He could have sworn everything was fine, even good, until one moment it suddenly wasn't. What had he done wrong?

Not that it mattered now. She wanted him to leave, and he couldn't do that without getting his wallet.

Jeremy finished buttoning up his shirt, stepped over the small pile of her earlier outfit, and walked back to her bedroom, pressing the heel of his hand into his groin. *Damn it*, he repeated silently before raising his other hand to knock.

His knuckles stalled in the air and he moved closer, turning his head so he could hear better. Was she *crying*?

Well, shit. He'd never been able to turn his back on a crying girl. When he'd seen Bonnie Pearce sobbing over her dropped ice cream cone back in second grade, he'd given her his, even though he'd saved up for what seemed like ages to buy it. Ever since, a woman's tears were like the sucker punch from hell, which was probably why his ex-wife had ended up with their house, even after cheating on him.

And this time, the tears might even be his fault.

Jeremy picked his way over to Taralynn's kitchen. Good thing she'd left a light on near the door or he might've given himself away, stumbling around in the dark. He opened her freezer, grabbed a paper carton, then slid a couple drawers open and closed until he found a spoon. Bonnie Pearce might have been the start of his weakness, but that experience had also taught him a near-guaranteed fix.

Back at the bedroom, he rapped his knuckles on the door and nudged it open. Taralynn sat up in bed, her eyes widening as she pulled the blanket in tighter around her. Streaks of gray trailed down her cheeks.

"I, uh, forgot my wallet," Jeremy said, reaching the ice cream he'd found out to her.

She frowned. "You went in my freezer?"

He shrugged and set the pint of mint-chip on her night-stand, then added the spoon on top. "I was doing something way more intimate not five minutes ago."

It didn't take him long to find the missing wallet, a dark lump on her pale rug. He slapped the leather into his other palm, meeting her gaze again. While he'd been turned away, she'd smeared the mascara trails into two big gray smudges. "Sorry I turned out to be so, uh, disappointing." *Oh, what the hell.* "I am willing to learn, though," he added with a small smile.

"Just go," she said, not returning the smile.

He nodded, shrugging again.

"And don't forget the NDA," she called after him as he strode back out the door.

Chapter Three

HEAT ARCED THROUGH TRACY'S BODY, and she shifted in her chair to dislodge the memory of Jeremy's touch. Her fingers hovered over the keyboard the way her hero's lips hovered over the her-oine, waiting for Tracy's command.

Sunlight streamed through the gauzy curtain behind her computer. A homemade mocha cooled in her I TURN COFFEE INTO BOOKS mug. But even a week after her aborted attempt at a fling, echoed sensations sent a shiver through her insides. His mouth closing over her breast, or his tongue playing over that one spot on her neck, his hands gripping her hips…

What would it have felt like, if she hadn't stopped him? Would he have been as good as the scenes she wrote?

Probably not.

Like it or not, Tracy wasn't Taralynn. She never could've lived up to his expectations—and he almost certainly wouldn't have lived up to hers.

Just tell me what you like.

Tracy stretched in her chair, lifting her hands up over her head, then exhaled sharply, dropping her arms. Her fingers skated over the waiting keys. Over the last few days, she'd written some decent steamy scenes, but she couldn't quite figure out this character, with his office job and calloused hands. His deliberate skill but superficial confidence.

But unlike real life, on the page she could fill in the gaps however she wanted. As soon as she built a character profile she liked.

A light rap on her door saved Tracy from the demanding expectation of the blinking cursor. She uncurled from her seat and crossed the living room to crack the door open.

She jerked back at the sight of Jeremy's crooked smile. Was she imagining him there? His gaze swept down her body, taking in the faded tee shirt with its stretched-out collar, dipping off one shoulder, and her lilac terrycloth skirt. Had she even brushed her hair before clipping it up out of her way?

Nope, no trace of Taralynn here.

Jeremy's smile ticked up as his eyes met hers. "Can, uh, can I come in? I promise not to go anywhere near your freezer."

Hours she'd spent, fantasizing about the near-stranger standing in front of her. But letting him back in after he'd clearly heard her crying, without even the cover of Taralynn?

Metal jangling from down the hall made up her mind for her. Nosy neighbors didn't need to know anything about her life—professional or personal. She stepped back and swung the door open, then quickly shut it behind him. "What are you doing here?" she asked, leaning against the door as if her heart weren't beating out some fast-paced dance to which it didn't know the steps.

The sunlight filling her apartment picked out red and blond undertones in his hair and the couple days' worth of stubble on his jaw. His hand came to the back of his neck, and he shook his head at the floor, like he couldn't believe he was there, either. When his eyes met hers again, he looked a little queasy. Or maybe that was her, projecting. "No one's ever kicked me out of bed before."

Beyond a fleeting quirk of her brow, Taralynn didn't react to his admission. Jeremy had tried to move on, to forget it. She was only one woman. But this woman was basically an expert on sex, and he'd apparently performed so horribly he'd made her *cry*. And not in that good catharsis way. He had to know where he'd gone wrong.

"Listen,"—he cleared his throat—"I get you have high expectations, but I'm willing to learn." He took a step forward, but she tensed, flattening her palms on the door behind her.

Jeremy moved back, and the paper bag he held smacked him in the leg. He offered Taralynn a smile and lifted the bag toward her. "I, uh, I have a gift for you, or for us, if you're up for…"

Her stony expression didn't budge. He let the bag drift down. "Okay, I get it. Sorry." He sighed. "Well, then, would you mind," he asked, pulling out the book he'd also tossed into the bag, "signing this, maybe? For my coworker, who told me about your books. She'd never forgive me if I didn't at least ask."

The sight of her own book seemed to spur Taralynn into action. She smiled stiffly and straightened from the door, reaching for the book. "Sure, of course. What's her name?"

"Naomi." She'd dropped a book on Jeremy's desk a couple weeks after his divorce was official, then bugged him until he broke down and read it. She'd insisted he borrow book two as well. Then he'd bought or borrowed all the rest.

Taralynn strode past him to the desk that stood against her window and sat down to sign. After she let the pen drop, she bent to a set of cubes beside the desk. The oversized tee shirt slid further off her shoulder, and Jeremy glanced away.

He hadn't paid it much attention last time, but her living room setup was pretty unremarkable. A couch with a couple extra pillows, bookshelves, and an oval coffee table, all in light colors. Welcoming, easygoing, and entirely at odds with the sultry, seductive image in his mind of Taralynn Harwood. Then again, so was how she looked today. Though the curves of her breasts were evident even under the loose tee shirt, he'd never have imagined the woman at the desk as a temptress, expert in all manner of sexual techniques, games, and fetishes. Way more informative than the *Kama Sutra 101* book he'd bought after his divorce.

She crossed back toward him and held out a small bag with her TANTALIZED BY TARALYNN branding printed on the side.

"Thanks." His fingers brushed hers as he accepted the bag.

She crossed her arms under her chest, highlighting the fact she wasn't wearing a bra. Probably on accident. "I can sign one for you, too, if you'd like," she offered with another tight smile.

"Oh thanks, but, I feel like enough of an idiot already, barging in on you." The fantasy he'd had of getting her to relent, to teach him everything she knew about pleasure, now seemed better suited for one of her books than anything he'd actually do. Even if he had, in fact, come there. Maybe she'd feel more comfortable out in public, and actually talk to him. "If you haven't eaten, I've heard great things about a diner that's not far. Some good food might even be enough to replace all your embarrassing memories of me." He shot her another smile for good measure.

Her jaw shifted slightly as her eyes skimmed down his body. Something seemed to convince her, and her arms dropped to her sides. "Do you remember the NDA you signed?"

Jeremy shrugged. He hadn't exactly read it carefully. "Think I got the gist." And he wasn't going to be running around sharing his utterly shameful performance.

She walked around the coffee table and reached for a folder on her bookshelf. "So you know what you signed," she said, handing him a fresh copy of the agreement.

Might as well go for broke. "Maybe you should explain it to me over breakfast," he countered.

A light chuckle puffed out of her lips, accompanied by a tiny eye roll. "I'll need to change." She paused, watching him like there was more she wanted to say.

"You look pretty great from where I'm standing," he offered.

That got him a bigger eye roll, but a light pink washed over her cheeks. With a small sigh, she added, "If we're going to have breakfast, you should probably know my name is Tracy."

Chapter Four

RESEARCH, THAT WAS ALL IT WAS. When again would Tracy have a chance to experience sitting through a casual meal with a man while the blend of memory and fantasy made her want him badly enough she almost didn't care about all the witnesses surrounding them?

She stirred some sugar into her iced tea and took a long sip, leaning back in a wicker chair out on the restaurant's patio. The June day was marvelous, even picturesque, with rare white clouds in a bright-blue sky and plenty of people milling around the nearby shops, or striding down the sidewalk hand in hand. Even still, the weather couldn't claim responsibility for the touches of heat caressing her body. No, some combination of Jeremy's presence and Tracy's own imagination was to blame for that.

"So," she said once a waiter had taken their order, "remind me, what is it you do?"

Jeremy set down his coffee and laced his fingers together. Tracy shrugged away the memory of his calluses scraping lightly against her breast.

A self-deprecating hint of a smile appeared before he answered. "I'm in marketing analytics."

All Tracy knew about marketing was how grateful she was to be able to pay someone else to analyze all those numbers and charts and reports nowadays.

"Nowhere near as exciting as your work, I imagine," he added in her silence.

"Oh, I don't know." Tracy picked up her iced tea again to help diffuse the awkwardness. What had she expected, coming out with him? She of all people knew how much work the sparkling conversation of a great romantic match took to create. "We probably spend a similar amount of time staring at a computer screen." She forced her lips into a polite smile.

"There is that," he said quietly.

They watched each other silently across the edges of their cups, their eyes occasionally pulled away by a passerby but always tugged back to each other.

Finally the waiter appeared with their food, lifting some of the tension. Except the food arriving meant that short of a fortuitously timed phone call or a horribly transparent excuse, they still had to spend an entire meal together.

At least the sexual charge had more or less disappeared. Apparently that had been mostly her fantasy after all.

"Looks pretty good," Jeremy said, his knife arcing toward Tracy's crab cake Eggs Benedict. His hands stilled, utensils hovering over his own combo breakfast. He wasn't wrong—both plates did look good.

Tracy picked up her fork and stabbed a cube of melon from the small bowl nestled near the edge of her plate. Jeremy sliced through his omelet, the movement drawing her attention again as she popped the fruit in her mouth.

Her imagination might have taken creative license, building up the heat between them, but he definitely used his hands for something more than office work. She took another bracing sip of tea before venturing into conversation attempt number two.

"What kinds of things do you do outside of work?" she asked. When he looked up from his plate, she added, "Unless marketing is much more hands-on than I thought."

"Oh, uh…" His gaze fell back down, and he turned one palm up, like he'd never thought much about the calluses. "Woodworking, actually." He met her eyes again, nodding a couple times. A tinge of self-assuredness had subtly shifted his posture, infused his expression with a fresh touch of warmth. Was he thinking of the same moment she'd been remembering?

"Is that like carpentry?" Tracy asked, carefully slipping her fork into the hollandaise-drenched edge of one crab cake. Carpentry could be an interesting line of work for a future character, so maybe this breakfast actually *would* count as research.

"Sort of." Jeremy nodded again, not that she could see him, her attention on her food. "Carpentry is more about building something, putting pieces together into a sturdy, functional item. Woodworking is about…" He paused. He'd never really had to explain his hobby to anyone before. His ex-wife had preferred he keep it all out of sight in the workshop. He finally settled on, "Details."

Tracy'd perked up from earlier, when the conversation had felt like pulling teeth, or some less clichéd way she'd describe it. But confusion quirked her eyebrows toward each other. "I'm not sure I understand."

"Well, let's see. If we're talking about building or installing kitchen cabinets, that's carpentry. If those cabinets have carved doors, like a vine or something around the perimeter, that's woodworking. Or…" *What else?* "Figurines made from a block of wood, that's woodworking too. I guess it's more artistic, in a way. Like the difference between a gate with simple vertical and horizontal bars, and a wrought-iron gate. Not that carpentry isn't hard or important,"—he shrugged—"just not what I like to do."

Tracy's head angled to one side, the breeze playing with a wispy strand of her blonde hair like it wanted to caress her cheek. "So what is it you like to do?"

"Oh, I'm still experimenting with different pieces, less of the standalone figurines except for practice. I actually…" He drained the last of his coffee to wash down the embarrassment creeping up his throat. Woodworking was something he did for himself, not something he talked about much. "I've started putting some things up for sale, but I haven't really zeroed in on a niche yet." At this point, woodworking was somewhere in between a hobby and a career aspiration. He'd even gotten a commission for a custom trunk a little while ago. But artisanal work wasn't exactly in high demand, and he wasn't exactly a master, either.

"You like it better than your job, though," Tracy said.

No question there. "What makes you say that?" Now that

she actually seemed to be looking at him, instead of the distantly polite gaze of before, what was it she saw?

"Just how you talk about it." Her head tilted to the other side as she sized him up, a tiny smile tugging at her lips. "Like it's something you really care about, but are scared to share."

It was a little unnerving to have a stranger see into him like that. But then, it was probably a side effect of being a writer. "Is that how you feel about your work?" he asked to get the conversation away from the sense of rightness he felt, eliciting something beautiful from the lines of the wood.

Her lips parted, fresh pinkness coming to her cheeks. "Sometimes, especially with something new." A little spaniel passing near them on the sidewalk caught her attention, and her lips found an easy smile. It changed into something more closed off when she looked back to him. "Taralynn doesn't really have that luxury."

Right. It was like he knew she was a writer, but he hadn't quite put Taralynn's books together with the woman sitting across from him. But Tracy *was* Taralynn.

"What made you decide to use a pen name?" he asked.

"Oh." A hand lifted to hide her mouth as she quickly chewed the forkful she'd just taken. "When I started, it was partially because of how scandalous it was, writing romance, especially"—her voice lowered, mock horror filling her face—"erotic romance."

Jeremy caught himself mirroring her smile.

"Even today," she continued, a bit sad, "women lose their jobs because the wrong someone finds out they dare to write romance."

His smile dropped away. "That's awful." But then, even Naomi felt compelled to defend the choice to read the genre. It didn't seem like a stretch that that stemmed from the same type of judgmental B.S. that could cost someone writing it her job.

"It is." Tracy lightly shrugged the topic away. "Plus, my real name just isn't memorable," she said, making him chuckle.

"The name might not be, but you sure are."

Her chin ducked and one eyebrow lifted in a look that would have put any schoolteacher to shame. "You really do read a lot of romance, don't you?"

Jeremy grinned. "Being cheesy doesn't make it less true."

Jeremy seemed like a blend of contradictions, with his self-conscious hesitations yet confident insistence. Pieces made sense—like his deft, assured handling of his utensils, since he worked with his hands—but not enough to give Tracy a clear enough picture for the character she'd started drafting.

He brushed against her side as he maneuvered out of the way of someone coming past them on the sidewalk, and Tracy swallowed at the resulting flicker of warmth, skimming her gaze from his shoulders and down. She jerked her eyes back to the street ahead of them. She was being ridiculous.

"Will you forgive me one more question about your writing?" he asked as they neared her building.

"Sure," she said automatically. She should do a better job remembering he was a reader first, and anything else second— or not at all.

"The things you write…"

"Yes?" she prompted, even if she was pretty sure where he was going.

His eyes found hers, filling with a blend of intensity, curiosity, and that discomfort that came when people weren't sure if they were about to get too personal. "Are they taken from real life, your life?"

Tracy smiled patiently at the question she'd been expecting. Not everyone had the courage to ask, but pretty much everyone assumed the old adage of "write what you know" applied literally to her books, or really all erotic romances.

"Some of them." The practiced answer came easily, and it always served her well. People didn't need to know the scenes she meant were things like her public embarrassments, her self-consciousness and sense of inadequacy when she found herself overly sweaty in public—always on her face, the one place she couldn't actually try antiperspirant—or realized too late that she'd missed a spot shaving.

Jeremy's gaze darkened as his mind undoubtedly jumped to some personal favorite from one of her stories. He wasn't thinking of the awkward, imperfect, realistic touches she gave her characters. People never did.

His eyes dropped away, landing briefly on her breasts. Had his thoughts moved on to imagining doing all those things *with* her? He had already seen her pretty much naked.

Tracy cleared her throat, resetting her purse on her shoulder. If Jeremy were imagining anyone, it was Taralynn. And if there were one place Tracy could never be her, it was in bed.

At least the reminder made it easy to pull herself together as they stopped in front of her building. "Thanks again for brunch," she said.

"My pleasure." Jeremy paused, the lips whose feel she remembered all too well parting just enough to show he wanted to add something. Whatever it was, he thought better of it and took a small step back. "Thanks for indulging me." Those lips pulled into a smile tinged with regret. "I'll see ya around."

Chapter Five

THE CARPENTER WASN'T BEHAVING. Tracy'd even considered making him a woodworker, but it felt too obvious. Even if the temporary title of the story was "Working with Wood." She couldn't keep that, anyway. It was just too on the nose.

Not that it would matter if she couldn't figure out what he wanted. Both he and the heroine were waiting for Tracy to get writing—so they could get to the scenes where they would get it on. But the blend of willingness and inexperienced hesitation wasn't easy to work with. It was like he was up for anything, but where could they *start*? She'd already aged the heroine a few years, to help the slight teacher–student dynamic. But he didn't feel completely inexperienced, either. Just vanilla enough to think he knew it all, when really there was so much more to discover. Like the kinkiest thing he could imagine trying was a threesome, even if the idea made him nervous enough that he'd never actually do it.

It wasn't like the heroine had tried it all yet either. She'd just been a bit more adventurous in her past, the kind of woman who felt comfortable taking her time in sex shops and was up for exploring all sorts of toys. This story was going to be pretty light on the kink, it seemed.

Something niggled at Tracy's memory. What kind of toy would this heroine pull out with someone she'd never actually had sex with yet? Something to ease him in but that wouldn't be too predictable for Tracy's readers...

She pushed back from her desk and stalked across the living room, into the kitchen to make a fresh cup of coffee. She paced as it brewed. Maybe it was time for a field trip to the local sex shop, like the one Jeremy had stopped by before his unexpected visit.

Wait. He'd left his little bag of goodies, but she'd never actually looked. What had he bought to try and entice her into bed? She grabbed her coffee and went over to the cube organizer where she stored all her Taralynn reader goodies. Sweet Sexation's simple paper bag lay right on top. Tracy upended it onto her desk.

Out fell a pair of furry azure handcuffs with wide reinforced wristbands and a four-pack of edible body paint. Pretty tame, all things considered. But it definitely fit with a hero who was in a little over his head with the adventurous sex he thought he wanted to explore. It wouldn't be the worst idea, having her heroine tie the hero up and tease him with delicate brushstrokes foreshadowing the strokes of her tongue. Or she could paint strategic parts of her own body to direct the attentions of his mouth where she wanted. Still pretty tame, but with some delayed gratification, it could be an interesting first encounter for them.

Tracy dropped the cuffs back into the bag and picked up the paints. Passion fruit, strawberry, chocolate-caramel, and mint, all in vibrant colors that looked toxic even if the paints weren't. A small business card had landed underneath them. She flipped it over as the paints rejoined the handcuffs.

A lovely wooden coffee table in a complex combination of infinity shapes featured on the front, with only a website printed underneath. It had to be Jeremy's work. He'd scribbled his phone number in one corner, too.

Tracy switched from her story file to a web browser and typed in the site address. Skipping the section with his bio, she clicked over to the photo portfolio. There weren't too many pieces, maybe a couple dozen at most, but they were beautiful. The warm lighting of the photos helped. Some included zoomed-in shots of the details, often flowers or vines. One table had carved legs shaped like puppies on their hind legs, reaching toward the tabletop. There were a couple kitten bookends, too, like he didn't want to commit to one side of the pet debate.

A few photos included prices for those interested in buying. All out of her price range, of course. She was lucky to make enough from her books not to need a side hustle, but artisanal one-of-a-kind furniture was still the kind of luxury she couldn't justify. Even if it would have made for a nice memory. Or a bittersweet one.

By the time the story was done, her hero would have only the bare minimum in common with the man she'd met. Surface features, sure, and Jeremy's hobby would become her hero's career, but otherwise he'd be a figment of her imagination. Eventually, she'd know her hero better than she knew the original.

She tapped the business card on the desk and switched back to her draft, leaving Jeremy's website up for future reference—*research*.

At some point she'd have to look into the details of wood-working, learn some of the ins and outs to add a little realism. If not for how they'd met, Tracy would've called Jeremy to help with the technical info, maybe asked for a tour of his work-shop. If he had a workshop. It didn't seem like he'd be doing this kind of work in a spare room.

And it didn't matter, anyway, since she couldn't call him. Touches of the real Jeremy might be good inspiration for this one story, but that was it. The original belonged firmly in her memories. No matter how often those morphed into fantasies.

Chapter Six

"HOW DID I NOT KNOW ABOUT THIS? And why did no one *tell* me?" Danica wailed as Tracy joined her critique partners for their monthly meeting.

"Tell you what?" Tracy asked, setting down the brownies and gluten-free, dairy-free fudge she'd brought before plopping onto Jana's armchair.

"About the horrors of buildup and 'miracle' of clarifying shampoo," Chantal commented. She double-checked the label on the fudge before grabbing a piece.

"What?"

Jana scoffed, coming out from the kitchen with a frosty bottle of white wine. "Don't get her started."

Danica held up her flawlessly manicured index finger. "No. I am traumatized." She fixed Tracy with a "you'd better listen to me" stare. "Have you seen how gross buildup can get on your hair? My hairstylist pulled out her scissors and scraped off all this white crap I didn't even know was there, or *could* be there. No one ever told me!"

Tracy laughed as the others exchanged eye rolls. "Sorry, Dani. You know I'm a wash-and-wear kind of girl." She didn't even bother with hairspray if she could help it.

"Exactly!" Danica leaned forward triumphantly. The others groaned, passing around the box of brownies and filled wine glasses. "You *think* you're safe, that you're fine with your shampoo or conditioner, but turns out, you can wind up with this disgusting coating on your hair that makes it dull, and prone to tangling, and generally gross."

"In conclusion," Nyah broke in, "get yourself some clarifying shampoo. Can we move on?" She leaned back on the dark-green couch, tossing a chunk of brownie into her mouth.

Danica huffed and crossed her arms, slumping on the other end of the couch. Tracy frowned, trailing a lock of hair through her fingers. Clarifying shampoo sounded like a good idea, if there was really some kind of unseen coating making her hair "generally gross."

"Agreed, let's get to the 'bitching about our writing' part of the agenda," Chantal quipped, sending a round of chuckles through the group.

"I'm stuck on my legal fury trio," Jana offered. "I keep thinking of new holes in the premise."

"What do you mean?" Nyah asked. "I thought you had it figured out."

Tracy took a sip of wine then leaned forward for a piece of fudge. They'd started bringing gluten-free, dairy-free options for Chantal, but in the process, they'd discovered an awesome local allergen-safe bakery with some delicious go-tos.

"Well if they're three out of hundreds, then how did these

three end up living together? Or is it like a fury crash pad, and they're the ones rotating through?"

"Can't they just be assigned?" Danica asked, switching from pouting to problem-solving.

"Little dedicated teams for every big city," Chantal added. "Wait, is this a BDSM trilogy? Are furies all tops, punishing the bad, bad humans?"

Tracy chuckled as Jana blushed. They all wrote at different heat levels, and Jana was supportive, but the hottest her books got was fade-to-black. Kink of any kind was outside her comfort zone.

Nyah laughed too. "This is sounding like prime spin-off potential."

After a few more jokes, they all refocused on the writing. Helping each other work through craft and business issues was ostensibly why they got together monthly, though the main priority was actually getting all of them out from behind their computer screens to combat the isolation of being an author. Online communities helped, but nothing beat some face time with people who actually understood the author life. Like looking up something about adult film laws only to get sucked into a sex worker research rabbit hole. Normal people just didn't get that.

When they'd killed a second bottle, Chantal turned to Tracy. "You've been quiet today. What're you working on now?"

And there it was. For a couple hours, she'd forgotten about the carpenter and his real-life counterpart. Tracy scrunched her nose and downed the rest of the wine in her glass.

"It can't be that bad," Nyah said, holding out the remaining brownies.

Tracy smiled but waved the dessert away. "I just can't get a handle on this new character. It might not even be worth pursuing." Maybe the memories really were better left for her fantasies, no matter how much she'd tried to spin the time with Jeremy as research.

"What's the premise?" Chantal asked.

"A carpenter, eager to expand his sexual horizons but with no idea what he's gotten himself into. But so far all I have are some middle-of-the-road sex scenes."

"That doesn't sound like you," Danica said, her forehead wrinkling in concern.

"Why a carpenter?" Jana added. "Pretty sure the wood euphemisms don't even count as a double entendre at this point."

The others exchanged a series of incredulous looks as Tracy's face heated. "I might have met this guy who dabbles in woodworking. Thought it could turn into something, a story, I mean, but—" She shrugged off the rest of the thought.

"Sounds like someone needs another dose of inspiration," Chantal teased, gyrating her hips to underscore the point.

Even Jana looked thoughtful. "Men spent centuries convincing beautiful women to sleep with them by calling them their muses. Turnabout seems fair."

"Plus you have the perfect excuse," Danica piled on. "Ask him to show you his work."

"Yeah, he can show you how he handles his tools," Nyah said with a wolfish grin.

"Are you really pimping me out for a book idea?" Tracy asked.

Chantal's hand came to rest just below the little golden fox dangling from her neck. "The things we do for our art."

"And no one's saying you have to sleep with him," Jana assured.

Danica raised the hand with her wineglass. "I am. I'm saying it." Six months after her divorce had been finalized, she didn't feel comfortable getting back out into the dating world herself yet. "And then write one of your hot, hot stories so the rest of us can live vicariously."

"Oh, so you're pimping me out for *your* benefit," Tracy teased as Jana got up to take the empty bottle to the kitchen. "Got it."

"And yours," Danica protested. "This is what we call a win-win."

"Pretty sure you should be counting the carpenter," Nyah said dryly.

Danica shrugged. "Okay. A win-win-win."

Tracy just shook her head as her friends laughed. Maybe contacting Jeremy for a tour of his workshop wasn't the craziest idea. If she was going to write this story, she'd need to learn enough about carpentry to help the character seem realistic. Seeing Jeremy in his element might help inspire her, like Jana said. It wasn't like they had to sleep together for him to be her muse. She just needed something more to go on.

Chapter Seven

"HI, JEREMY, THIS IS TRACY MILLER. I was wondering if you would consider showing me around your workshop and answering some more questions about carpentry and woodworking, if you have the time. I'm happy to treat you to lunch in return. Hope to hear back from you soon. My number is..."

Jeremy smiled and hit the key to play the message again, like a complete dork. He'd struggled to put Tracy out of his mind. Naomi coming up with new questions to ask about Taralynn wasn't helping. He tried to answer as vaguely as possible, careful not to cross the line into describing Tracy.

Even though they were, technically, one and the same. Both versions kept popping up in his dreams. Sometimes even together, like naughty and nice mirror images.

Sexy as it was, Jeremy shook the image out of his head and called the number she'd left. If she wanted to see him again, that meant he hadn't completely blown it. Was she reaching out only to research something for a story, or was that an excuse? Either way, he could show her around the corner he rented of a shared artisan workspace. Maybe break past some of her defenses over the lunch she'd suggested. Hanging out with Tracy, showing her some of his latest designs, seemed like the perfect way to spend a weekend afternoon.

Tracy ran her palms up her legs, checking one last time for anywhere she might have missed when she was shaving. Not that there was anything she could do about it now, sitting in the parking lot outside a large warehouse that had apparently been reworked into an artists' workshop. For a Saturday, not many cars stood in the asphalt lot. Jeremy had suggested meeting out front, but he wasn't there yet, so Tracy flipped down the driver's-side visor to double-check her makeup.

She resettled the clip holding part of her hair back, swiped under her eyes for stray bits of mascara, then rolled her eyes at her reflection. She was only here to get a better sense of what woodworking was, nothing else. Jeremy had no reason to think this was some kind booty call, right? Because it *wasn't*.

Still she passed the wand of her peach gloss over her lips and surreptitiously sniffed near her armpits. *Deodorant: check.*

By the time she flipped the visor back up, Jeremy stood outside the door to the workshop, which was now propped open. With one last sharp exhale, Tracy switched out the lip gloss for a small notebook, smoothed her top as much as the seat allowed, and got out of the car.

Jeremy's eyes found her quickly in the nearly empty lot, and he grinned. She stifled the urge to make sure her skirt hadn't somehow accidentally gotten tucked into her panties.

Stopping a couple steps away from him, she said, "Thanks for doing this."

"My pleasure," he murmured, gesturing inside.

High windows let light into a large room haphazardly separated into workstations of varying sizes, and with varying degrees of privacy. A nearby corner seemed dedicated to large tools, a circular saw the only one she could name.

Jeremy's palm brushed her back just long enough to get her attention. Tracy turned to find him so close she had to tilt her chin up to meet his eyes.

"Shared tools," he explained. "They can be reserved in advance, or used by anyone if they're not reserved. It's one of the main perks, that we don't have to invest in all of the big equipment individually."

"Do you use them often?"

"Whenever I have to handle large pieces of wood." The corner of his lips edged up.

She smiled back. "That's the only one of those you get."

"Given the context that might be…" He smirked again before smoothing his expression into an imperfect poker face. "Difficult."

She turned away so her amusement wouldn't encourage him, wandering deeper into the workshop.

"We get all sorts of projects here," he said, stepping in beside her. He looked good today, in jeans and a heather-blue tee shirt tight enough to show off his build but loose enough to still look casual. "Metalworking, sewing, even painting. Jewelry-making. Anything people don't have space for or don't want to do at home. Some people just like the atmosphere, and spaces can be rented out for different amounts of time."

The barriers cordoning off different workspaces grew higher as they walked, offering only glimpses of people's work. Most had cabinets with locks hanging from the handles or sheets thrown over workbenches.

"There's a kitchen-slash-break room of sorts in that corner, and I'm over here." He nodded to the last section in the back, which was essentially the entire back corner, sectioned off by one and a half temporary walls that stretched up a couple feet above them but left a gap across from the kitchen area. Clear plastic tarps covered wood stacked against the cinderblock wall.

Jeremy stopped near the edge of the gap, close enough to her that a new charge filled the air, along with a hint of spice. His head tilted toward his workspace, part invitation, part challenge.

You're here to work, Tracy reminded herself as she stepped past him. The touches of heat dancing through her insisted otherwise.

Jeremy shook his hands out, following Tracy inside. He'd first rented this space because his ex-wife had refused to deal with all the wood chips and dust anywhere near her home. It hadn't taken long for him to feel more at home here than at their place, and the access to the workshop's tools was really helpful.

But no one else had ever come here, aside from some of the other folks renting adjacent spaces. This really was *his* space, away from work and any outside pressures to be someone specific, fit into whatever box people wanted him in at any given time. He didn't have to think about anything or anyone except whatever he was trying to make.

Now Tracy stood by his workbench, inches away from the carved table legs he was working on. Sunlight from the high windows streamed in over the tops of the impermanent walls, glinting off her golden-blonde hair when she moved. She wandered over to the shelves where he kept his tools and picked up a gouge, testing its weight in her hand as she glanced at him over her shoulder. "Looks dangerous."

"If you don't know how to use it." Jeremy leaned back onto his main worktable, curving his fingers against the edge.

"So what are all these for?" She put the gouge back and rose on tiptoes to get a closer look at the top shelf.

"Are you really writing a woodworking character? I mean, if I'm not allowed to make the obvious jokes, how are you going to avoid it?"

"Creativity. And it might be carpentry." She slid a pen out of the spiral binding in the little notebook she held. "Are the tools very different?"

"A bit, yeah. There's less precision." He crossed his arms as she jotted down notes, peering at everything he had. "I heard one expert describe the difference as one eighth of an inch. Small enough that it doesn't matter much for carpentry, but it can ruin a piece in woodworking."

"What are your favorite tools?" she asked, bending slightly to look at the tabletop panel waiting to be carved. He'd sketched out a simple vine pattern, but lately he'd been thinking about rounding out the edges, softening the lines from the standard rectangle.

Like the soft curves of the woman who'd moved on to his shelf of practice pieces. Meaning all his pieces, really.

"Gouges, chisels, knives. Some people use power tools, but aside from cutting the wood down to size, I try and do everything by hand."

"Wow, really?" She still hadn't turned back around, but that just gave him more time to watch her. There was nothing

Taralynn about her today, with her floaty skirt covered in little pastel flowers and her hair clipped loosely back. She flipped it off one shoulder, baring her neck before reaching toward one of the smaller figurines on his shelf.

For a Saturday, the shared workspace was unusually unoccupied, with only Kiara in her alcove, putting the finishing touches on her first commissioned wedding gown. The entire building was silent enough to forget it was a shared space. And the corner Tracy was in was entirely protected from view, anyway.

Something about her examining his work kept Jeremy in place. Was she seeing the mistakes—the uneven hooves, or the asymmetrical features? His ex would have rolled her eyes and turned away by now, bored by his amateurish attempts when they could have bought something that looked better. She'd never understood why he bothered trying to create something with his own two hands.

Tracy set down the unfinished little stallion and picked up a bear he'd made to practice carving something as detailed as fur. She cradled it gently, like it was fragile, valuable, trailing one fingertip along its back.

Tracy slid the pad of her fingertip over the intricate texture of the bear's fur, smooth in some places but rough in others.

She should have done more research, so she'd have something moderately intelligent to ask. If this were a story, this would be the moment the hero came up behind her, trapping her body between him and the shelves, brushed her hair aside, started kissing her neck… Or if this were her carpenter and his *tutor*, she would jump up on one of the tables and proceed to give detailed instructions for what he had to do before being allowed to touch her. And what he was allowed to do once he did.

But this wasn't a story, so all Tracy felt was awkward. She let the bear settle back in its spot. When she turned around, Jeremy was watching her, waiting for something.

"So what are you working on now?" she asked, stepping a-round him to look at the bits of wood, tools, and even sketches on the center worktable. Everything in his section was kept fairly neat, organized but not compulsively so, with only a hint of wood dust lingering in the air.

He moved closer, reaching across her to an untouched block of wood. "Trying to turn this"—he paused to pull a carved piece from under a sheet of paper—"into this. They're supposed to be table legs, if I can get them similar enough."

Her mind was looking for anything remotely sexy. That was why seeing him hold a long piece of wood carved into smooth curves sent a flash of heat through her. His hands had transformed the sharp, uninteresting angles of the first block into something that now, with his fingers cradling it, looked almost sensual.

When she finally looked up, a touch of that warmth lay deep in his eyes. "Show me," she said, then cleared her throat to get rid of the hoarseness.

Confusion blended with his amusement. "You want to watch me work?"

"Like I said." She swallowed past the dryness. "Research."

It would be easy. He could let the blocks drop and turn just enough to put his hands on her ribs, lift her up onto the work-table. Kiss her until they both forgot to breathe. In the fictional version, his workspace would be outside so they could feel the sun on every inch of exposed skin. Which, eventually, would be every inch. Kissed by the sun before being kissed by him.

"Whatever I can do to help," Jeremy murmured, snapping her back to the present. He went over to the corner with his display shelf and began methodically clearing things off the smaller table beside it.

Get it together, Tracy. Shrugging off the fantasy hovering at the edge of her mind, she turned back to the sketches and bits of wood beside her. Loose sheets featured designs in different stages of completion, different versions, even some with markings on top of a finished sketch, all pinned down by the four pieces of wood—the half-finished table legs.

"I don't have an extra seat, so this will have to do." Jeremy's palm rested on the cleared surface.

Tracy walked over without a word, stepping close to leverage herself up onto the makeshift seat. His jaw bulged, his head dipping down toward her, but when he moved, it was away to the shelf with his tools. She dropped her purse beside her and turned to a fresh page in her notebook, not that she'd filled the last.

Jeremy laid out his selection of tools to the right of the stool and shifted one of the untouched blocks to the center. Then he stripped off his shirt, dropping it on the far corner.

"What are you doing?" Surprise cleared the breathiness from her voice.

When he turned to look at her over his shoulder, his expression could be described only as smoldering. "This is for one of your books, right? What hero would keep his shirt on as he worked, especially when he's showing off for a woman?"

"One whose tools could gouge flesh as easily as they do wood."

He turned back to his work, and Tracy bit her lip, briefly shutting her eyes against the wave of desire that one look had sent through her.

Nonchalant, he balanced one of those tools in his fingers. "A tee shirt wouldn't help me much if I made a mistake like that."

She swallowed again, tapping her pen against the notebook. "Do you normally wear something else?"

"Normally, I try to avoid stabbing myself with my tools." A woodchip arced into view, proving the muscles in his back were moving not only for show.

"This is a terrible angle for watching you work," Tracy pointed out, though the view was anything but terrible.

Slowly he set everything down and twisted on the stool to face her. "Is watching me ruin a block of perfectly good wood really what you want to do?"

Chapter Eight

JEREMY HADN'T IMAGINED THE HEAT in her eyes. She hesitated to answer long enough that he got up, and her lips fell shut. He could have kept working, but with her watching him, every cut was coming out wrong. A few more and he would have had to toss the block, find a replacement. It wasn't what his hands wanted to be doing.

Their silence grew heavier with every step he took toward her. The little notebook fell easily from her grasp, and he set it aside. Her neck arched as she looked up at him. He nudged her knees open to move closer, the soft material of her skirt effortlessly making way.

Cupping her jaw, he waited, giving her time to hit the brakes before things went further. Not that tearing himself away now would be any easier. With a little exhale, she shifted toward him in silent but unmistakable permission. He'd been fantasizing of touching her again for so long that the kiss didn't stand a chance of being gentle. But she didn't shy away, her lips parting for him, her tongue meeting his with a ferocity that was more battle than dance.

Her hands skimmed up his sides, and he broke away from her mouth to taste the soft skin behind her ear. Her fingers dug into his muscles, pressing him closer as he trailed kisses lower. He palmed her breast, and her leg crooked around his thigh. With a low growl, Jeremy recaptured her reddened lips, slipping both hands up under her top. His thumbs swept against her taut nipples, and a tiny gasp interrupted their kiss, her leg pulling him flush against her.

Shifting his arm to support her torso, he kissed down her throat to the tops of her breasts. His other hand slipped inside the lace of her bra, cupping the lush weight of her as his tongue traced a languid pattern on her skin. Her hips shifted, her breath growing rough. Her free leg also wrapped around him as she arched backward, encouraging his lips lower.

He pulled back to release the fabric in his way, fingers fumbling in his haste to unclasp her bra. She let him go to tug the straps down her arms, but clarity seeped into her eyes, and she glanced away from him to the workshop.

"No one can see you but me," he assured. Even if someone came into his space unannounced, which they wouldn't, Jeremy's body shielded her from view. It wouldn't if he sank down to his knees, slipped under her skirt, and finally got to taste her. But there was time for that.

Her gaze jumped back to him, and he bent for a softer kiss, trailing a finger down her spine until it caught on her top.

She reached beneath the hem to pull out her bra. He didn't see where she dropped it, the outline of her freed breasts pushing against her top far more deserving of his attention. But the press of her legs around his hips had lessened, the momentary distraction dulling the spark of her desire.

Threading his fingers through her hair, Jeremy caught her lips again, starting slow this time.

The soft brush of Jeremy's lips gave way to a nibble, then retreated again to those frustratingly gentle flutters. One hand kept her head angled up for him, but his other fingers encircled her breast, so close to where she wanted them but immobile.

After the next nibble, Tracy snaked her tongue out, but he pulled back, tugging gently on her hair so she couldn't follow him, deepen the kiss. Didn't mean she couldn't do something else. She slid her palms up his torso, over his chest, pulling his neck back down to her. He obliged, his tongue tracing along her bottom lip. One hand slipped down his abs to his belt, and a quiet growl sounded deep in his throat, his fingers tightening around her breast, but his grip on her hair eased. She leaned into the kiss, grazing his bottom lip with her teeth before dipping her tongue inside. She traced the line of his waistband with one fingertip, keeping her touch slow, methodical.

He gave in first, tongue twisting with hers, the kiss growing urgent as his calluses scraped against her nipple. Her legs tightened around his, and the bulge under his jeans notched against her, turning everything inside her molten. Tracy barely held back a whimper, her hips instinctively pressing closer to him.

He pulled down the strap of her top, baring one breast as his fingertips teased the other, driving her to distraction. She braced one arm behind her on the table, her head falling back as he kissed down her chest. His teeth caught her nipple first, fingers pinching the other with matching pressure. A slow lap of his tongue eased the light sting but intensified the aching need, and Tracy writhed against him. Strong fingers molded the weight of her breast as his lips closed around the tip, sucking gently twice before taking her deeper, tongue swirling around her nipple.

Air prickled along her skin as he kissed across to the other side, hands falling away to slip under her skirt. His palms skimmed up her thighs, and he nuzzled her top out of his way to tease her other breast. Fingers crooked around the straps of her panties, and he stepped back, her legs dropping to give him room. His mouth fell away as he bent lower, tugging on the fabric beneath her skirt.

Tracy reached out for his shoulder, her fingers digging into the solid muscles as he lowered to his knees, exposing her torso to the natural light streaming in through the workspace's windows.

"Wait," she moaned, her mind catching up as her panties started to slip away. They were practically in *public*. "No, wait," she repeated, letting go to resettle her top and cover up.

This time he heard her, freezing. His hands released their grip on her panties, cupping the outside of her hips. Tracy shifted back on her perch so she could bring her knees together without whacking him in the head.

Confusion seeped in through the desire in his eyes, and he sat back on his heels. "What's wrong?"

Tracy shook her head. They'd gotten carried away. *She'd* gotten carried away.

His hands skimmed down her thighs as he let go, pushing back up to his feet. He crossed to the worktable, hands curled into fists. But when he turned back to her, it wasn't anger in his expression. "What did I do?" he asked, pained desperation for an answer underlying the words.

"Nothing," she exhaled. "It's nothing you did." None of this was his fault. She just couldn't be what he wanted.

Jeremy nodded, not that he believed her. They'd both been into it, until suddenly she wasn't. So it had to be something he'd done wrong. He turned away to pull on his shirt, then leaned against the table, gripping the edge again so he wouldn't make even more of a fool of himself. Like he always did around her.

Tracy was tucking her bra away in her purse, her nipples still pressing against the fabric of her top. He forced his eyes up to her face. Her lips were slightly swollen, reddened and all too tempting.

"At least I know I can kiss well enough," he tried to joke. It came out tense.

Her eyes jumped to him, but whatever she was going to say melted back behind a stoic mask. Her fingers tapped unevenly against a little box she'd taken out of her bag to make room for her bra. She slid off the table, smoothing her skirt down with one hand, and picked up her purse. "I should go," she said quietly, stopping beside him. Two more taps and she offered him the box. "I brought you this, to say thanks for…"

Jeremy reached a hand out to accept. "You brought me lube?" Sometimes following her thoughts was like jumping from a mountaintop into the ocean. Impossible to get your bearings.

"In case you've never tried silicone…" She trailed off again with a little shrug. "It's safe and it lasts, and it's less sticky when it dries."

"Right." He set the box aside. "Thanks for the tip."

"I'm sorry if—" The thought ended with a sigh, regret trickling through that unflappable shell.

She'd cried last time. He'd been so bad he made her cry. Would she cry again once she made it to her car?

"I'll tell you mine if you tell me yours," he ventured quietly. Maybe then he'd at least understand where he'd gone wrong.

"My what?"

"Secret." Something close to panic flashed on her face, too fast for him to be sure. "You're the one protected by an NDA," he pointed out. "Hell, I'll even go first."

She held his gaze for a moment that stretched until the air around them felt brittle.

"All right," she finally said. Her lips pinched in a frown as the sound of Kiara's sewing machine reminded they weren't actually alone. "But not here."

Chapter Nine

"MAKE YOURSELF COMFORTABLE," Jeremy said perfunctorily as he let Tracy into his apartment, but nothing about this was comfortable.

She hugged her purse tighter, stepping past him into the airy living room. Unsurprisingly, most of his sparse furniture was wood. The space would have been inviting if not for the awkwardness blanketing the two of them.

Before they'd left the workshop, she'd ducked into the bathroom to put herself together. Amazing how something as simple as having her bra on helped her feel more in control. Or had, until she'd come back out to the waiting Jeremy. They'd walked the several blocks to his apartment in silence. She could have demurred, just gotten into her car and left, but something about his need to talk had tugged her along. Maybe if he unburdened himself he'd feel better, and she wouldn't feel so guilty.

"Get you a drink or something?" Jeremy offered. "Please," he added, gesturing to the brown leather couch.

"Some water would be great," Tracy said with a tight smile. What was she *doing* here?

He disappeared, and suddenly the room felt lighter. Tracy went over to the staggered floating shelves that held a collection of books interspersed with some more of his figurines, including the kitten bookends he'd showcased on his website. Most of the titles seemed to be reference books about woodworking and marketing, with some biographies. So this wasn't where he kept any copies he might have of her books, or he'd stuck to ebooks.

She returned to the couch, perching on one end with her purse in her lap. It was easy to picture this place with a happy couple in it, curling up on the couch to watch something on the TV, or play a board game, or even just read in companionable silence. The round wooden table in one corner could hold a colorful vase with fresh flowers, or maybe a fruit centerpiece. They'd eat some meals there, but probably just as many off the coffee table in front of her.

The opposite corner, the one by a door that probably led to a bedroom, would be the perfect place for a little desk, right under the windows. He could build something small but comfortable—a little workstation, the type that would have once been used for writing letters or paying bills but could be ideal for anyone needing to do some simple work from home. Some added seating would make the living room perfect for the occasional intimate friendly gathering. The room would soak up the laughter like it did the couple's love.

The picture fell apart as Jeremy reappeared, holding glasses of ice water. His face was drawn, the touch of sadness worming its way right into her heart. Tracy unclenched her fingers from her purse to accept a glass. He moved away to pull one of the dining table chairs to the other side of the coffee table, but he leaned his elbows on the back rather than sitting down.

"We don't have to do this, if you don't want to," Tracy said as a bead of condensation rolled down to hit her fingers.

He nodded, contemplating his own water. He took a sip and stepped away to set the glass on a windowsill. Back at the chair, he wrapped his fingers around the top. "So I'm divorced," he said, "which isn't any kind of a secret."

With a sigh, he dropped down to his elbows again. Tracy set her glass on the single corkboard coaster waiting on the coffee table.

"We were married for almost five years, together awhile longer than that. Everything between us was fine, you know?" His eyes found her again, asking her to buy into this image of their marriage. "We had normal spats, but no big arguments. Our parents liked each other. We had a nice home and things we liked doing together, but also space to do our own things. Everything was fine," he repeated.

Tracy nodded despite the undertone of denial. This was his big secret—divorce? Or that he hadn't seen it coming?

He straightened, his palm scraping roughly across his mouth. A bitter laugh escaped him as he turned and took a couple steps away. "I can't believe I'm about to tell you of all people this," he muttered under his breath.

"Me of all people?"

He spun back toward her. "She cheated," he said, chin notching up defensively. When Tracy didn't say anything, he deflated. "I thought maybe counseling or something would help. She said it was a relief that I finally knew. She'd met him months after we met, and they'd been sleeping together on and off most of that time."

"That's awful." Tracy would never understand why people did that. If his wife had wanted to be with someone else, or even with both of them, why not be honest about that? Give everyone involved a choice.

"Yeah, well. The day we signed our divorce papers she told me the truth." He grimaced at the memory. Shame lined his face, weighing down his shoulders. "Turns out, she kept going back to him because I'd never satisfied her. Never even given her an orgasm. At least with him she didn't have to fake it."

Tracy's mouth popped open. "Jeremy, come on." She slid the purse off her lap and stood, rounding the coffee table. The single chair remained between them like some kind of shield. "You were married for years, together for what, the better part of a decade, and she never once mentioned that she wasn't satisfied by your sex life? That's not on you, it's on her. I mean, assuming you aren't secretly horribly abusive." A possibility, maybe, but that didn't seem like him, for whatever Tracy's impression was worth. "Look, more than likely, she was just lying to be cruel."

He nodded but not like he believed her, bitterness twisting his lips. "Women never fake it, right?"

"Of course they do," Tracy allowed. "So let's say she was telling the truth, that she'd really never had an orgasm with you in all that time. Cheating still wouldn't be the solution. You see that, right? Communicating would be. You can't fix a problem if she's actively convincing you there isn't one."

Pensiveness deepened the two small grooves above the bridge of his nose. But whatever he was thinking, he shook it away. "Well, whatever the truth is." His hand came up to rub the back of his neck. "After the divorce, my friend Naomi, the one you signed a book for? She gave me one of your books. She was joking when she said it'd help me know what women want, but I wasn't when I read them. Studied them, I guess. By the time I was with someone new, I'd learned everything I could."

As he spoke, his previous assuredness shifted back into place, though it felt a little hollow now. He shot her a crooked smile. "Your level of sex play may still be out of my league, but I've never second-guessed my ability to please the woman I'm with again." He shrugged and added, "Until you, anyway. But I really am willing to try whatever you want. I'm open to anything. Just tell me. What am I doing wrong?"

Anger swept away any trace of guilt she might still have felt. "So, what, I was your final exam? Give Taralynn Harwood an orgasm, and you never have to doubt yourself again?"

Her words knocked him back a few steps, his eyes rounding. "What? No! I... Maybe," he admitted, frowning as if surprised he was saying it. "That first night we met, maybe. And I knew it would be fun, with everything you know. But that's not why I came back."

"You came back because you failed, and you couldn't stand that." Humiliation burned through her, overtaking the anger. She'd been nothing more than a challenge he'd set for himself. Not even a human being, someone to have some fun with, but a *test*. She spun away to pick up her purse.

"Tracy." He followed her, stopping shy of the coffee table when she glared at him. "I like you," he said, the earnestness almost believable. "Whatever it was at first, maybe I didn't even understand myself. But that's not what this is now."

"This? This isn't anything," she said, heading for the door. She paused with it open in her hand. "Here's a secret for you, Jeremy. Taralynn and Tracy are different people. The one you want? She doesn't exist."

Tracy didn't wait for a response before wrenching the door closed behind her. And whatever Jeremy had wanted, he seemed to know better than to follow. By the time she reached her car, all the anger and embarrassment had made way for an all too familiar wave of disappointment.

The real secret, the one she couldn't believe she'd even considered telling him? Apparently she'd be taking that one to her grave. Just like her virginity.

Chapter Ten

JEREMY GRIMACED WHEN HIS LAST dart barely made it onto the edge of the board. He stomped toward it and started yanking out the little projectiles.

Gus hooted behind him. "Looks like someone's off his game!"

In more ways than one. Jeremy passed the darts off and slid back into his seat, pouring himself a fresh beer from the waiting pitcher. He used to enjoy these weekly nights out with his coworkers, chatting over drinks, playing darts or pool, almost always going home with a pretty woman who'd joined their group over the course of the night. It was easier picking someone up in a casual atmosphere, chatting until their respective groups dispersed and they were the only ones left. Everyone knew what they were getting themselves into, and he *never* disappointed. Not anymore.

Not until Tracy.

He scowled, taking a measured sip so he wouldn't down the whole glass. He hadn't *meant* to treat her like some kind of prize. But how stupid would he have to have been to say no to a night with Taralynn? Back when he thought she *was* Taralynn. Didn't mean he hadn't been drawn to Tracy, too.

Tracy, who was Taralynn but wasn't. As if that wasn't confusing.

"What's up with you lately?" Naomi asked, twirling the little plastic stick in her cocktail.

"Dry spell?" Chris guffawed, his elbow twitching in Jeremy's direction like they shared some joke.

It had been weeks since Jeremy had gone home with someone. Ever since he'd first met Tracy, it hadn't felt right. He didn't want to be in bed with someone and unable to give her his full attention. And lately, all his attention was on Tracy. She dominated his dreams, leaving him hard and aching. And pissed off, knowing he'd screwed something up and didn't have a clue how or what to do about it. He couldn't even talk about it, thanks to that damned NDA. So she was stuck in his head, bouncing around in an endless loop.

She was mad he'd gone home with Taralynn that first night, but it wasn't like Jeremy had even *known* about Tracy at that point. Both versions tortured him in his dreams, the sweet Tracy with her floaty skirts and shy laugh, and the sexy, self-assured Taralynn. The angel and the siren, both tempting him to do everything he hadn't had a chance to with the real one. Everything that would send a man to hell if heaven was reserved for the chaste. It would be worth it.

The one you want? She doesn't exist, Tracy had spat out before stalking out.

But she was wrong. He wanted all of her, the real her. The one he'd laughed with, touched, kissed... Not like she'd been playing at Taralynn all that time. No, it was Tracy he'd tasted,

Tracy whose little gasps had encouraged him. Whose sighs echoed in his dreams as he sank into her.

She might think he'd just wanted to prove something, to check a box and move on. Maybe, at first, she'd even been right. But one time didn't seem anywhere near enough now to get her out of his system.

Not that he'd even get the once.

"Mind if we join you?" a woman asked, coming up to their table flanked by two friends. All pretty, all holding drinks, all probably happy to hang out with their mixed group long enough to learn who was up for some late-night fun.

"By all means." Chris sank back against the booth with a self-satisfied grin.

Gus forgot the dart game and rejoined their group as well.

"Please," Jeremy said, grabbing his glass and standing. He needed to get out of here. His bad mood shouldn't ruin their night. Leaving his spot for one of the women, he walked over to the end of the bar, cradling his beer. He'd finish it and go.

Naomi wouldn't be put off that easily, though. She came up beside him and rose on tiptoes to settle on an empty stool. Her chin plopped into one hand, elbow resting on the bar. "You okay?"

He grunted a response, not wanting to lie. Not allowed to tell the truth. Not that he'd learned anything worth keeping secret as it was. What was Tracy so paranoid about? Her name?

Naomi's shrewd eyes narrowed, but she didn't make any of the stupid jokes the guys would. "Women trouble?"

"Ain't it always," Jeremy said and sipped his beer like it wasn't anything important.

"Tried apologizing?" she asked, mirroring his casual sip before setting the glass aside.

His lips twisted bitterly. "How do you know I'm not the one owed an apology?"

"'Cause you're a squishy little teddy bear who forgives women even when they don't deserve it, and definitely before they've even asked."

He couldn't even argue. And it wasn't like Tracy owed him any kind of apology. She probably hadn't meant to work her way under his skin and latch on, stoking his curiosity along with his desire.

Jeremy sighed. "You good getting home tonight?" he asked Naomi.

Concern crooked her eyebrow but she nodded.

"Good." He pushed his half-finished beer away. "See you tomorrow," he murmured, bending down for a quick hug before making his way out into the chill night air. The Taralynn Harwood novel waiting for him at home was a poor replacement for the woman behind the words. But maybe if he finished it, tonight she wouldn't haunt his dreams.

Chapter Eleven

TRACY FROWNED AT THE SCREEN, slumping in her chair. This new story was fine, even if it was missing any kind of spark and felt a little repetitive, like a mosaic of her other books. But that could be fixed after the first draft was finished.

So why was she still stuck on the carpenter story she'd moved to her "unfinished" folder? Out of sight, out of mind had always worked before. And she'd never had a shortage of characters waiting in the wings for their turn to find love. It wasn't like that draft had been going especially well—that was why she'd moved on in the first place. The fictional version had been even more of a disappointment than her misadvised attempt at a fling with Jeremy.

She hadn't heard from the live version in the weeks since she'd stormed out of his apartment, and that was just fine too.

So why was she feeling so out of sorts? Boredom, maybe.

Reflexively her fingers saved the file, and she pushed up from her desk. One of the caramel-fudge brownies she'd picked up yesterday would help her get out of this funk. And maybe she should switch gears and read something to refill her creative well. Ignoring the hot chocolate mix on her counter—full on wallowing in this bizarre mood wouldn't help her book get written—she flipped on her electric kettle and set one brownie on a saucer.

Scraping and muted voices sounded in the hallway, but Tracy ignored those too, breaking off a corner of the brownie. She nudged it around on the plate with her fingertip, waiting for the water to boil. Only a few minutes stood between her and cuddling up on the couch with tea, the brownie, and one of the books waiting in her library queue.

A few minutes and the scratching that persisted near her door. She took a step toward the hallway just as it stopped. Shaking her head, she turned back toward the kettle and brought down a mug. Maybe she should go with an herbal infusion, something relaxing but with enough of a boost to brighten the day.

A loud thump nearly made her drop the mug, her fingers catching it right before it could hit the edge of the counter.

Okay, enough. Sure, the hallway was shared space, and if she hadn't already been in this weird mood, she'd never have said anything. But whatever was happening out there, it could happen near someone else's door. Or, well, anywhere else that wouldn't interrupt her reading time.

She stalked to her door, paused for a deep breath and to paste on a calm smile, then yanked it open. And found Jeremy, fidgeting with a sheet-covered something at his side.

He jolted upright faster than she could shut the door. Her smile slipped effortlessly into a frown more befitting her mood. It had been *weeks*. What the hell was he doing here?

✧ ✧ ✧

"Uh, hi," Jeremy stammered out, awkwardly resting his hand on the sheet he'd been fiddling with as he went over and over the apology he'd prepared. The one he'd entirely forgotten the moment Tracy'd surprised him, opening the door before he'd even managed to knock. She didn't look happy to see him, not that he blamed her.

"What are you doing here?"

"Before you justifiably slam the door in my face…"

Her eyebrows lifted impatiently as he trailed off.

"I made you something," he said lamely.

Discomfort flashed in her eyes and she shifted backwards, gripping the door like she was trying to figure out if she could lock it faster than he could push his way in.

Jeremy sighed, taking a step back so he wouldn't be crowding her. "That's not what I meant to say." Why did he always sound like an idiot around her? "I'm sorry—"

An older woman shuffled past him, grumbling about them blocking the hallway.

Tracy rolled her eyes, shaking her head a little, but opened the door wider. "Just come in."

"Right, okay." His head bobbed on his neck as he swallowed. Running his palm across the top of the gift he'd brought helped center him. Jeremy focused on crouching to slip his hands under the top edge and lift. Tracy watched him warily but stepped out of the doorway so he could maneuver inside her apartment.

She waited by the shut door, watching the sheet-covered panels of wood instead of looking at him. But showing her was easier than talking. Jeremy tugged the sheet out from where it had gotten pinned under one edge then slipped it off, balling it up in his hands. He hugged the beach ball–sized lump as her eyes grew wide, her lips popping open.

Almost instantly her stance softened, her head tilting as she took in the piece he'd been working on over the last few weeks.

"Wow," she breathed before meeting his eyes. "That's amazing."

Something in his gut unclenched. Even if he couldn't get his apology out, if she never wanted to see him again, at least this piece of him would be some part of her life, the way her books would always be a part of his.

The bookshelf was beautiful. He'd shaped it like an open hardback, just standing vertically, even having each half swell like the gentle wave of the paper. Shallow grooves covered the top and the side closest to her, mimicking the sheets. Tracy wandered closer, letting her fingers trail over the top. The shelf only came to her hips, wider than it was tall, maintaining the proportions of an open book.

Jeremy was still clutching the sheet to his abdomen, but he'd relaxed a bit as she examined his gift. The tiniest smile touched his lips, like something had been settled between them. "I made sure the outer edges were still deep enough for mass markets," he said, somehow proud of his work and seeking her approval at once.

Tracy stopped fondling the beautiful wood and shifted away, keeping the shelf between them. He'd even carved little grooves on either edge of the "spine" in the back panel. Because that was the kind of attention he paid to his art—and this was definitely art—even knowing the shelf would likely stand pressed against a wall, leaving the back unseen.

If she kept it, which she probably shouldn't.

"Why would you bring me this?" Tracy asked, crossing her arms.

He shrugged. "I made it for you. I, uh." He twisted away, gesturing toward the far corner of her living room, empty except for some boxes of books and miscellaneous reader swag she sometimes put there if it didn't fit neatly in the cube organizer by her desk. "I noticed you had the space, and I wanted to make something you'd like. A shelf seemed more practical than some random figurine or something."

"Definitely more practical," she agreed. *And really thoughtful.*

"I can help you move it over," he offered, "if that's where you want to put it. Or somewhere else." His shut his eyes as if chastising himself internally. His jaw shifted, like he couldn't find the words. The care he'd taken with the shelf did a lot of the speaking for him.

Tracy let her weight settle into one hip, dropping her hands. "I guess, technically I still owe you lunch…" In exchange for him showing her around his workshop.

The tension nearly vibrating through his shoulders released a little. "No, you don't owe me anything. I'd like to have lunch with you, though. But, maybe we could talk first?"

Chapter Twelve

JEREMY'S KNEE BOUNCED AS HE SAT on Tracy's couch, waiting for her to finish fiddling in the kitchen. She brought out two mugs, set one on a coaster in front of him, and lowered to the end of the couch, angling her body toward him.

Ignoring the coffee, Jeremy twisted toward her too. "Listen, I'm sorry."

Her gaze drifted down to the cup cradled in her hands.

"I was so twisted up, so worried that I kept doing something wrong. Maybe I really did forget in the moment, to think of you as you, not as some kind of, I dunno. Proof, I guess. That she was wrong, or that even if she wasn't, I had reached some kind of..." *Shit.* He hadn't meant to get into any of this. Just to apologize, give her the shelf, and leave. But now that he was here, he didn't want to leave. At least not until she told him to.

And she wasn't, yet, her expression somehow patient and implacable at once. She wouldn't forgive him just like that, but she was giving him a chance he didn't want to pass up.

"Ever since my wife said... Well, you know." Jeremy's hand scraped over his lips as the words sorted themselves out. "I guess I've been trying to get to some point where I was good enough to pursue something serious with another woman. I wanted to be sure I'd never fail her, in that way at least."

Tracy's expression had shuttered, a frown tugging at her lips.

"No, that's—" Jeremy's hand reached for her, but he redirected it to the back of her couch. "I think, when we first met, it was a little bit like proving to myself I was *skilled* enough to move forward. And I hated that I failed. But I didn't mean to treat you like some kind of symbol. And I really do like you, Tracy."

She scoffed, taking a sip of her drink.

"I get why you wouldn't believe that. But I swear, all that only came up when we'd—" If there was a tactful way to say this, he wasn't able to find it. "When we'd stop. It wasn't something I was thinking about when we talked, and it has nothing to do with how attractive I find you. And I mean you, as you, not just that Taralynn persona."

He paused, trying to catch the thread of what he was really trying to say. "I'm sorry if I made you feel like you were some challenge, a test I was trying to pass. And I understand if you'd rather cut your losses. We definitely don't have to have lunch if you don't want." He picked up the coffee and slumped against the couch. His eyes fell on the wooden book he'd made, the crumpled sheet sitting on top of it now. "The shelf was just something I wanted you to have."

Tracy sipped her tea in a pathetic attempt to grab some extra seconds before responding. Something about Jeremy seemed so earnest, waking up that niggling guilt inside her. She could remind him that every sexual partner was different, wanting and enjoying different things. That people in good relationships still had to explore and learn what their partners liked. That communication mattered as much as, if not more than, skill.

But really, who was she to talk?

She'd come so close to telling him the truth before. What would it be like, for someone to know the secret that hung over her? Even her friends didn't know. Past a certain age, everyone assumed abstinence was either a religious mandate or some kind of defect—like it had to mean no one had ever wanted you. It couldn't simply be a choice.

Not that it was as straightforward as all that, either.

"It really wasn't you," Tracy murmured. "*Isn't* you."

He huffed out his disbelief like she had moments ago.

She leaned forward to slide her tea onto her low table, replacing the mug with a pillow she hugged to her chest. "You ever wonder why I had you sign the NDA that first night?"

He shrugged. "Figured it had something to do with your name."

"Well, first, I guess I should remind you that it's still legally enforceable." The words sounded cold, but she had to at least protect her career.

"You don't have to tell me anything," he said, also setting down his mug.

Anxiety tingled through her, making her lungs work harder to breathe. Tracy squared her shoulders with her exhale. "I've never had sex."

He chuckled, his lips quirking into a sarcastic slant. "Right."

"No, really," she persisted. In for a penny and all. "That's why I kept stopping us…you. Because I never have." Some part of her refused to say the word *virgin* aloud.

Jeremy's expression sobered as he watched her. "I don't understand."

Every rational part of her brain told her not to put words in his mouth, not to guess what was coming next. But still, she knew.

"But your books... You, what, use a ghostwriter?"

It would have hurt worse if she hadn't seen it coming. This way the pain of the insult just fueled Tracy's anger as she shot up from her couch, stalking away before rounding on Jeremy as he gaped up at her. "That right there? That's why you signed an NDA."

It didn't matter that she wrote every word of her books herself. Or that readers consistently complimented the spiciness of her sex scenes as much as the story overall. If even the suggestion of Tracy—*Taralynn*—being sexually inexperienced came out, everyone would claim she was lying, that her words weren't her own. That at the very least someone else had to "help" her write *those* scenes.

Even Danica had written a story with an aspiring romance writer whose virginity was some kind of handicap that prevented her from being able to write her book. It was a common trope, authors who wrote it conveniently ignoring all the sub-genres of romance that didn't include any sex in the first place. Outside of historicals, people often portrayed virgins as incapable of understanding anything about relationships, or of handling anything else about life on their own, either. Because of course a person couldn't be a full-fledged, functional adult without having had sex.

So a virgin writing award-winning *erotic* romance? The mere speculation about whether Tracy wrote her own books would be enough to take her career down in flames.

Jeremy's palms came up, surrendering to her fury. "I didn't mean to insult you," he said slowly, also standing. "But, how can you—"

"Right. Authors create entire civilizations out of their imaginations. They sink into the minds of serial killers, without ever having killed anyone. Any of a million details in a story rely not on personal experience but on a combination of research and creativity. And yet what we're categorically unable to divest from the author as a person are sex scenes.

"If it's a woman writing, anyway. Men writing sex tend to be nominated for awards, and somehow no one ever asks them if those disappointing experiences they portray on the page are a reflection of their own pitiful performances in bed. But the moment a woman writes sex, especially *good* sex where everyone involved gets to enjoy themselves without being shamed for it, it's labeled 'mommy porn.' And everyone assumes that if she's writing about it, she must have done it.

"So we find it utterly unbelievable that a *virgin*"—she finally spat the word out—"can write good sex."

Chapter Thirteen

HE SHOULD HAVE BEEN DULY CHASTENED. And he was, sort of. He'd never meant to insult her, but of course the suggestion that her books weren't her own would have been hurtful. Disrespectful.

Still, Jeremy couldn't help but smile. The anger had let something loose in her, bringing a light flush to her cheeks, a powerful confidence to her stance.

And yeah, it made sense now, why she'd seemed so on edge with him. He'd assumed he was doing something to turn her off, something she didn't like. Or wasn't doing something she *did* like. Because he'd done exactly what she said, conflating the author with the books.

"You're amazing, you know?" he said now.

Her eyes narrowed on him like she was gathering steam for another round.

"Not because you write hot sex without having personal experience to draw from." Though, admittedly, that too. "But how thoughtfully you've analyzed all this, considering everything that feeds into our assumptions." She softened at that, so he took a couple steps closer. "Most people can't ever be bothered to look beyond socially conditioned preconceptions."

"To be fair," she said, "many romance authors and readers have considered and even studied the ridiculousness of how our society denounces positive portrayals of sex, especially when written by women. But even they tend to discount virgins when having these conversations, equating virginity with a more general naiveté or inability to participate fully in society. Infantilizing virgins even while proclaiming that virginity is nothing but a social construct."

Jeremy nodded, slipping his hands into his pockets. "I'm sorry I did exactly what you said, assuming you'd done at least most of the stuff you've written about." It probably didn't help that he'd met her as Taralynn first.

"Yeah, well." Something sad flickered across her face. "Sorry to burst your bubble." She turned away, taking only a couple steps before being halted by the shelf he'd built, still angled awkwardly between her couch and the door.

"I'll repeat that I think you're amazing, and obviously talented. But."

She spun back toward him, somewhere between curious about what he'd say next and preemptively peeved.

Jeremy smirked, moving past the coffee table and around the end of the couch until he stood in front of her. His hands landed on her shoulders, and he couldn't prevent one thumb from tracing over her collarbone. "You're also kind of an idiot," he said quietly.

She jerked backward, more shocked than offended.

"Virginity may be a social construct, especially as it pertains to the perceived value of women. But Tracy, the first time you do *anything* is different. Doesn't matter what it is, and there really isn't any way around it. Think of the first book you published versus the tenth. No matter how prepared you were, how well you knew what to expect... It's just different."

He came even closer, letting one of his hands slip into the loose bun that held her hair up. "And the thing is, you know that. You've written that." She'd had several virgin characters in her books. While each one had treated sex a little differently, she'd never lost sight of their first times being a *first*.

Her breathing had deepened, the undeniable awareness between them darkening her eyes even though an edge of wariness remained. But her hands came to his waist, resting over his tee shirt.

"It should go without saying, but we can go as slow as you want. And we can stop whenever you want. Even if you'd rather we stuck around first base for a while. Or hung out without touching." The last was almost painful to say. But he could keep his hands off her if he had to, if that was what she wanted. His thumb swept over her cheek as if to call him a liar.

Tracy sighed, the shift in her posture bringing her closer. Still Jeremy waited, letting her set the pace she was comfortable with. Praying she wasn't about to kick him out.

A rueful smile lit her expression as she tilted her chin up. "We're never actually going to have lunch, are we?" she murmured, pulling him closer for a kiss.

Something had shifted in Jeremy now that she'd told him the truth. Like now that he believed her hesitation had nothing to do with him, confidence had settled comfortably in his skin. Instead of trying to keep up with some imagined version of her, he took his time, kissing her slowly as his fingers threaded through her hair, threatening to pull out the hairband that kept it all up.

And even if it hadn't needed saying, and she'd never doubted he'd stop the moment she asked—he had, after all, more than once—something about sex not being an implied guarantee let her sink into his languid kiss, the hint of coffee lingering on his lips.

One of his hands trailed lightly down her spine and Tracy shivered, leaning into him. His lips broke away, finding that sensitive spot on her neck only he'd ever discovered. He sucked gently, hand slipping under her tank top, the heat from his palm urging her closer. She sighed, melting into the sensation of being pressed against him, of his hands roaming over her skin, his lips teasing her but always staying above her collarbone. Her fingers slid under his tee shirt, tracing above the waistband of his jeans.

Jeremy nipped her ear and stepped back. His hand lifted to the nape of his neck, pulling the shirt off in one smooth motion, exposing the defined planes of his torso to the sunlight. He cupped her jaw, breaking her eye contact with his abs. A cocky smile quirked his lips. He intertwined their fingers, ducking down to brush her mouth with a fluttery series of kisses as he maneuvered her through her living room.

He stopped with the couch at her back, pressing into her ass. Tracy leveraged herself up to sit atop the back edge, Jeremy's hands snaking out to steady her as she wobbled. The slight shock only made her blood pump faster. His palms didn't move from her ribcage as she twined her hands behind his neck, her feet behind his knees.

Sticking to his word about going slow, Jeremy simply kissed her again, his tongue nudging her lips apart, opening her to him. The faint pressure of his chest against her breasts unfurled tendrils of desire in her.

Reading her mind or maybe just moving things along, Jeremy palmed one breast, swallowing down her gasp. His breathing had grown rougher, but he didn't move the hand, fingers digging lightly into her flesh. He broke their kiss to ask, "How slow are we going?"

The same sunlight that caressed him, showing him off for her, made her hesitate. But they'd already done this part. "Not that slow," she said, her voice coming out raspy.

Keeping his eyes on her face, Jeremy bunched the hem of her top at her waist, teasing it upward. "This slow?" he murmured, lips close enough to feather her neck but not *quite* kissing.

Tracy exhaled, half-chuckle, half-frustration. She hitched her legs a bit higher, ankles pressing the backs of his thighs to encourage him. Still taking his time, Jeremy traced a pattern on her skin with his tongue. The bunched tank top reached the elastic band of the attached shelf bra. His thumbs slipped under, easing the pinch of the band even as her nipples tightened.

"Hands," he directed, tugging the top higher.

Tracy swallowed roughly, lifting her arms above her head so he could finally peel the fabric away. He tossed it aside before she could think to cover up, catching her fingers on their way down and setting her hands on either side of her hips.

"Hold on," he added as his touch skimmed back up her arms. One hand detoured to land between her shoulder blades as the other found her breast again. His knuckles scraped along her nipple, tightening everything in her core.

"So beautiful," he whispered, bending to tease his lips over her sternum.

She arched backward into his grip, the pinch of his fingers rewarding the motion. "Jeremy," she breathed, not really asking for anything aside from *more*.

Chapter Fourteen

JEREMY DIDN'T QUITE KNOW WHETHER to smile or groan at the thread of anticipation in her body, the slight pleading note in her voice. So he just kept going. Rolling her nipple between his fingers, he let his lips trail over the other breast, kissing in a generous circle around the russet peak that demanded his attention.

Her soft little sigh didn't hide the blend of impatience and desire that squeezed her knees around his hips. Who was he kidding? He wanted this at least as much as she did. His lips brushed the tight knot of her nipple then parted, letting his exhale finish the hint of a caress.

Tracy's hands spoke for her, one landing on his bicep, the other on his ribs, both silently urging.

Jeremy let his parted lips slip around the tip, smiling as her fingers tried to press him closer. His hand dropped to her hip, steadying her on the couch. His tongue flicked out, sending a tiny tremor through her.

"Jer—" she started to say, but a longer swipe of his tongue didn't let her finish.

He blew on the moistened flesh, grazed it with his teeth, offered another feather-light kiss. Only when an incoherent pleading sound caught in Tracy's throat did he finally close his lips around the taut bud. Sucked gently. Swirled his tongue around. Bit with a touch more pressure, then sucked her deeper. Letting her gasps guide him, Jeremy savored her until her hips rocked instinctively, uncaring that at any moment she could tumble backward.

A soft whimper accompanied his straightening. Her chest rose raggedly with her breath, as if he needed the added enticement. The slightly uncertain desire in her eyes hit him right in the gut. Fingers digging into the terrycloth skirt bunched under his hand, Jeremy recaptured her lips. The delicate friction of her breasts on his chest was its own torture, a reminder to focus. There was so much more of her to taste, starting with the other side.

Or maybe not. He dipped his hand under her skirt, brushing over the top of her thigh, seeking the heat he was already aching to sink into. His fingers never got that far.

Tracy tensed, her breath catching as she broke their kiss. That uncertainty was tipping the scales on her desire.

"Above the waist," Jeremy said, moving his hand to suit. "Got it."

Her tongue flicked over her bottom lip as she nodded. "For now."

He reclaimed that lip, nibbling at it so she wouldn't do something stupid like apologize for having boundaries. His hands trailed up and down her sides as they kissed, letting her come back to feeling instead of thinking. When her hands started moving over him, he shifted the kisses to her jaw, then her ear. He sucked and nipped his way down her neck, licked swirls over her collarbone until her impatience wriggled her closer.

Smiling, he shifted back enough to let his thumbs cover her nipples, massaging in small circles as his mouth came to the other side of her neck. She shivered at his bite, and he soothed the skin with another slow lick.

"More?" he teased, even if her little sighs had already answered the question.

At her breathy "yes," he turned his attention to her neglected nipple, straining toward his lips. He flicked his tongue against the tip. Hours he could spend on her breasts, sucking, licking, nibbling. His jeans had long since stopped being comfortable, but it was worth it. Listening to her breath deepen into uneven gasps, soft little moans. Coaxing those tremors from her.

A thought wormed its way to the surface, and Jeremy hesitated. His lips lingered, dropping kisses up her breast before he straightened. He cupped her jaw, letting his fingers dislodge the elastic that was barely keeping her hair up as it was. It tumbled free as he asked the question that had interrupted him. "Tracy, has anyone ever given you an orgasm?"

"Besides me?" she challenged, flashing an image through his mind of her spread on a bed, head thrown back, expertly working her body to climax. *Fuck.* Another fantasy he could only dream of seeing someday.

"Someone other than you," he confirmed.

Her teeth caught her bottom lip, and he knew the answer before she shook her head. "No."

"Deal breaker?" Tracy asked, loosening the grip of her legs around him.

"Are you kidding?" he countered instantly.

She shrugged, slipping her hands from him so she could cover up.

"Don't." The word stopped her mid-motion. Jeremy dipped his head for a soft, lingering kiss, then added, "Let me touch you."

"Where have you been these last few minutes?"

His brow arched at the word *few*, but he didn't let her get away with the joke, nearly burning her with his look. "You know what I meant." His thumb swept along her cheek. "Do you want to keep going?"

The muscles low in her abdomen clenched in protest at the mere suggestion of stopping. And she could stop him later if that changed. "Yes."

Jeremy's fingers spasmed in her hair, belying his calm tone when he suggested, "Bedroom?"

Tracy nodded, sliding off her seat. It wasn't like he hadn't been in there before. And it was warm enough outside that she'd shaved her legs last night, even if she hadn't been expecting anything like this. Despite being perfectly fine spending her days in pj's, she made her bed every morning to preserve some semblance of routine, so that wasn't something she needed to worry about. Was there anything especially embarrassing in her bedroom that she was forgetting?

"Hey," Jeremy said, breaking into her thoughts. "What has you thinking so hard?"

"No, nothing." Or at least, nothing sexy. She should have been thinking about the man standing inches from her, close enough that she could still feel his heat on her chest, her nipples nearly aching for his touch.

Shaking off the intruding thoughts, Tracy leaned into him, lifting on tiptoes for another kiss. Jeremy caught her against him, their bodies melding together as their tongues tangled. She nudged him toward the bedroom door, and they moved together—until it was their legs that tangled, breaking apart their kiss as they stumbled.

Jeremy chuckled as they steadied each other. He wove their fingers together, stepping out of her way enough that they wouldn't actually fall over as they moved. His heels struck the door, swinging it open, and he threw a look over his shoulder.

"Tracy." He brought their hands behind her waist and bent down again to drop kisses on her shoulder.

She half-hummed, half-moaned in response, the renewed friction between their torsos sending fresh curls of pleasure through her.

He kept them moving, rounding the foot of her bed. "Turn around," he said, coming to a stop in front of her dresser. His hands slid to her waist, nudging her around to face the mirror atop the wooden drawers. Tracy started to protest, but his hands came up to cup her breasts, thumbs swiping across the peaks as his teeth grazed her neck.

He pinched her nipples, the sensation rippling through her, and her head fell back against his shoulder.

"Open your eyes," he ordered.

Surprise made her obey, catching his heated gaze in the reflection. One arm circled her ribcage, pressing her firmly against his chest, the unmistakable bulge in his jeans. His other hand slipped under her terrycloth skirt, fingers dancing over the top of her thigh as he sought her core. She jolted when he slipped under her panties, finding the wetness he'd coaxed from her.

Her eyes drifted shut again—and he stopped. Her hips undulated in protest, but he held her in place, his fingers just out of reach. Satisfaction filled his expression when she opened her eyes again, another intimate caress following. Meeting her gaze in the reflection, he lifted his hand to lick her off his fingers, the pure eroticism of the action washing away all her anxiety.

He nipped her ear, murmuring, "Take off your skirt, everything."

"I will if you will," she breathed, some part of Taralynn peeking through.

His lips curved up at one corner. "Not yet."

Tracy swallowed but did as he asked anyway, kicking her remaining clothes aside.

Jeremy's palm slid down her stomach, finding the curls she kept only trimmed enough to feel under control. The rough fabric of his jeans pressed into her ass as a fingertip circled her clit, arching her into him. The faint touch continued as his calloused palm grazed her nipple and his mouth resumed its slow torture along her neck, her jaw, her collar.

Her breathing deepened, the growing touches of heat tempting her to shut her eyes again, give in to the sensations, but the challenge in Jeremy's gaze assured he'd stop if she did. There was a reason he'd chosen the mirror instead of the bed.

Chapter Fifteen

A PERFECT PINK CRESTED TRACY'S CHEEKS as she gasped, then bit her lip. Jeremy slid a finger forward over her clit, maintaining the pressure as he dipped lower. Her head dropped back again, but her desire-darkened eyes stayed focused on the reflection of his hand.

Her own fingers dug into his thighs, steadying her on her feet as her knees softened. She whimpered in protest when he took his hand away, but they were just getting started.

"Put your foot on the dresser," he suggested. She stiffened, but he waited as she processed the idea, running the back of his fingers along her hip, her thigh. Finally she moved, tentatively lifting her leg until her toes perched on the edge of the dresser. His arm tightened around her as he fought the jolt of need urging him to strip naked and hurry things along.

Instead he nudged her knee wider, opening her up to his touch and the mirror. Uncertainty flashed across her face, but before it could take root, he passed his knuckles back over her clit.

"Wider," he said hoarsely, and she shifted her foot over to give them both a better view.

He teased her with his fingers, playing at her entrance without slipping inside. She watched as if transfixed, her lips parted with her breath. Her hips shifted, rubbing against him, and he silently cursed the restriction of his jeans. Her breath caught when he thumbed her clit, releasing in a gentle moan, quickly followed by a more urgent sound. Watching her come apart might be enough to push him over the edge too. But not yet.

He gripped the inside of her raised thigh and relaxed the arm holding her up. "Don't move," he said, stepping away.

"What?" she breathed, the haze of desire slowing her reaction enough that he was in front of her before she could think to drop her leg.

His lips passed over her open mouth, trailing down her neck, her chest. A brief detour to each breast had her clutching his head closer. But Jeremy wouldn't be deterred. He pressed open kisses over her stomach as he sank to his knees in front of her, taking in the sight. "You're so beautiful," he said, not leaning closer. This was always where she'd stopped him before.

Sure enough, her fingers released his hair. "Jeremy…"

"I promise," he said, dropping a quick kiss to the thigh that was now over his shoulder. "I won't taste you until you tell me to."

The words should have been reassuring, but Jeremy's hands skimming her legs and ass as he looked at her, spread open before him, wouldn't let Tracy pinpoint why the promise felt devious. Already she was flushed with wanting, her legs weak from the double assault of his fingers on her and the vantage point provided by the mirror, letting her watch every touch.

Now his head blocked the most pertinent part of the reflection, but that didn't matter with the pure lust on his face. He turned his head into her thigh, kissing up from her knee until his cheek nearly brushed against her curls. His teeth sank into the flesh, tearing a soft cry from her throat. He laved the bite with his tongue, but true to his word his mouth didn't go where she both wanted and couldn't quite feel comfortable with it being. Even if he had technically already tasted her.

"You don't—" she started to say as his fingers flicked over her clit again.

"Don't what?" he asked, letting the tip of one finger dip inside as he pressed a soft kiss at the base of her belly. His other hand wrapped around her leg, keeping her in place, or maybe helping her stay upright at the waves of sensation he was sending through her.

"Don't have to," Tracy breathed as her hips rocked into his hand.

He froze, looking up her body to meet her gaze. "I want to," he said clearly, over-enunciating the words. "But I won't," he said more lightly, turning his face into her other thigh as his fingers resumed their gentle torture. "Until you ask me to."

Patient but unrelenting, a finger slid back into her as the nail of his thumb grazed her clit and his tongue drew patterns on her hip. Her muscles tightened around his finger, and he nipped the top of her thigh. Her hand slid back into the softness of his hair.

"Use your words," he teased, a devilish glint in his eye as he coaxed her hips into a rhythm with the gentle thrusts of his finger. He sat back, watching her writhing against his hand.

"Please," she moaned.

"Please what?"

Her muscles clenched again at the sight of him there, driving her to distraction with his hands but still waiting for permission to pleasure her with his mouth. Her eyes jumped to her reflection, unabashedly naked and on display for this man, her own gaze echoing the desire in his.

"Lick me," she watched herself say.

"Here?" he asked, his tongue tracing a line at the seam of her hip.

A part of Tracy wanted to whimper in frustration. But the woman in the mirror wouldn't plead—she'd command. "Here," she corrected, slipping her fingers into her wetness to show him.

Need sharpened his gaze as her other hand encouraged him forward. Both of their fingers moved away. Her head bowed back as his tongue slid over her in one long stroke.

Tracy's legs trembled, the hand on his head urging him on. Jeremy pulled back. She was getting close, but he wanted her to be able to let go completely when he helped her over the edge, at least the first time.

She didn't even protest when he stopped, panting as her head dipped to look at him, her hair falling forward to the tops of her breasts. His own lungs fought to pull in air, staring up at the erotic sight.

"Bed," he said, unable to form more than the one word.

She nodded, letting her foot slip down from the dresser. She stepped out of his grip, moving away toward the purple comforter on her bed. Her hips swayed with every step.

"Sit on the edge," Jeremy managed to say, forcing himself to his feet as well.

She faced him near the foot of the bed, hair loose, nipples tight, the slopes of her body illuminated by the light filtering in through her windows. All her earlier shyness had been replaced by a sultry assurance. "Jeans," she countered.

His dick agreed, tired of fighting the pressure of the zipper. Jeremy's fingers made quick work of the pants, slipping his socks off too but leaving his underwear for now. They weren't finished with her yet. And he couldn't wait to get back to the taste of her.

The thought hurried him around the bed, and he pulled out one of her pillows. "Sit," he repeated once he'd reached her.

This time she did. He tucked the pillow behind her, nudging her shoulders down onto it. Her hands caught him, pulling him in over her. Jeremy pressed one knee into the mattress and let his lips brush the spot under her ear that always sent a little shiver through her. Her fingers clutched at him as he kissed down her torso again. Bracing himself with one hand, he used the other to mold her breast, sucking at the tip, bowing her body off the bed. He switched sides, nipping at the sensitive peak until her fingers dug into his shoulders.

Her leg came up around his hip, encouraging him to skip the rest and slide into her *now*. Somehow he tore himself away, sinking down to the floor despite his body's protest. She jerked as his hands found her ankles, and he smiled, pressing a quick kiss to each knee. He met her gaze and moved each foot into place on either side of her hips, opening her to him once more. His self-control ran out and he spread her even further with his fingers, burying his mouth in her.

Tracy's toes curled at the edge of her bed as Jeremy's tongue bucked her hips. The sure strokes switched to feather-light teasing swirls, and back. His hands gripped her in place, anchoring her to the touch of his mouth as the rest of her hovered so close to the release her every cell begged for.

"Jer— Please," she whimpered.

His fingers dug into her hips, keeping her at his mercy. He sucked at her clit in little pulses, and her muscles contracted in matching rhythm. A strangled moan escaped as his teeth grazed her, nearly letting her fly.

Instead he leaned back, shooting her a cocky smirk as her fist hit the comforter.

"Jeremy," she repeated, not above begging but not finding the words.

"Hush," he said, and even his exhale sent a tremor through her. He held her gaze as a thumb stroked over her, followed by another little puff of air from his lips. "You don't really think," he said, pausing to flick his tongue out, "that I'm going to leave you here." He lapped at her with deliberate slowness, savoring every bit of her with equal attention.

Tracy's teeth sank into her lip, her body settling into the unhurried caress, her breath calming. Heated resolve darkened Jeremy's eyes, and he sucked at her once more, stealing the air from her lungs as everything sharpened to only her need and the man who controlled it. The pull of his mouth was interspersed with light scrapes of his teeth, the firm pressure of his tongue, a pattern she didn't care to decipher as long as he didn't stop.

Her head fell back, and Tracy gave herself over to the cadence of sensations Jeremy coaxed from her body. Higher and higher he took her, her need coiling tighter until finally he sent her soaring. Beyond breath, beyond thought, leaving nothing but the pleasure bursting through her. The surge of release broke into rolling waves that swelled from her center where his mouth lingered, guiding her through the flood until she floated back to herself.

Chapter Sixteen

TRACY'S EXHALE DRIFTED OUT OF HER and her feet slipped limply from the bed. Jeremy settled beside her, propping himself up on one elbow. Her eyes fluttered open, satiation leaving her languidly spread on the bed, the sight impossibly making him even harder.

His palm landed on her stomach, a tiny jerk tightening the muscles under his hand. Before he could ask if she wanted to stop there, she twisted, fingers gliding down his abs toward the elastic sitting low on his hips. His eyes closed, breath hissing out between his teeth as she brushed over him through the fabric that felt more like a torture device.

"Off," she said, and he was up like a shot, finally stripping himself bare. Her eyes zeroed in on his dick, which practically jumped at her attention. She sat up to reach for him, but Jeremy caught her wrist.

"I can't," he gritted out. Even the idea of her touch was nearly enough to make him embarrass himself. He'd recover, but… "I don't want to wait to be inside you."

Her eyes grew round, her hand dropping from his touch.

"Unless, you don't—" he started saying as she said, "Okay."

"Yes," she repeated and scooted to the center of the bed, pushing the pillow out of her way.

"Okay," Jeremy said under his breath, looking around for his jeans. Because jeans meant wallet, and wallet meant condom.

"Here," Tracy said, and he spun back toward her. A little square waited between her fingers.

Jeremy ripped it open and slid on the condom in record time. Back at her side, he paused, brushing her hair back behind one ear. "You sure?" he asked.

An irresistible knowing smile curved her lips. "Yeah." She reached for him, hands roaming up his torso, over his back as she lay down, pulling him over her.

Jeremy ducked down for a kiss, one hand palming her breast. He might be desperate to bury himself in her, but first he was going to do his damnedest to get her back to needing it too.

She rose into his touch, pressing their torsos together, opening eagerly for his kiss. Her legs hooked around his hips, and she wriggled beneath him, gasping when she brushed against the length of him. He rolled her nipple between his fingers, and her legs tightened, shifting him closer.

Jeremy levered himself up, giving himself space to watch her. He skimmed his hand down her body before gripping himself. He brushed his dick along her opening, coating it in her wetness, holding himself back when her hips rose in instinctual invitation.

Her fingers dug into his sides, but the impatience was tempered by the hint of tension that clung to her again. Jeremy circled a knuckle around her clit, reminding her body of the pleasure to be had. He'd be damned if he left her with only one orgasm.

"It's okay," Tracy half-moaned, running her palm up his chest. "I want this." Her hips wriggled again in confirmation. "I want you."

Heat blazed in Jeremy's expression, but still he didn't slide into her the way her body wanted. Tracy lifted off the bed enough to run her lips along his collar. He groaned by her ear but held himself still. So she let her tongue trail over his skin, pressed soft kisses to the straining muscle in his neck, stretched up under him to nip at his earlobe.

Jeremy shifted to place himself directly at her opening, pulsing his hips forward the tiniest bit, the contact a faint echo of what she wanted. He dropped his hand back to the bed, bracing himself above her, and Tracy let her shoulders fall back as well, holding on to him.

Instead of filling her fully, he pushed forward with a short stroke. Her muscles contracted around him as he pulled back, obviously wanting him deeper, but the small movement repeated. Was he afraid of hurting her? After a few more of the infuriatingly insufficient motions, Tracy's hips shifted with the stroke, trying to bring him where she wanted.

He stilled, a glint of something in his eyes, but she wasn't going to beg this time. Betraying her resolve, her legs urged him closer.

Another small movement of his hips, and another, each one deliberately even, repeating to drive her mad. Until suddenly he drove into her, stretching her even as her muscles tightened to hold him in place, the deepest part of her quivering around the hard length of him.

He pulled out almost entirely, and Tracy braced herself for another wonderfully long stroke—that never came.

Those even little movements resumed, the friction sending flickers of heat through her, teasing and torture at once. She scraped her nails along his back, but the steady rhythm continued, Jeremy's jaw clenched in concentration. As she was about to give in, to ask for more, he pushed into her again, two delicious, long, sure strokes that seemed to fill her down to her toes.

And back to the shorter ones. *Two, three, four...* He was *counting.* Anticipation sent a shiver through her, a garbled sound of breathless desire catching in her throat.

Sure enough, after seven he rewarded her patience with three long strokes. The muscles in his arms bunched as he continued the pattern, his determined control just this edge of unbearable. Six short ones, four long, coiling her earlier need even tighter, hotter, but not quite letting her reach that peak. As he started to pull out, Tracy's legs gripped him, trying to hold him inside her.

Jeremy shifted to run a calloused palm over her nipple, the sparks of sensation startling her into giving him enough room to move on to five short strokes—and five long. She couldn't help but count each one, her hips matching his unshakable rhythm, her muscles squeezing around him each time he withdrew. She tried to breathe through the four short ones, but her mind was on the six long—more than half now! Even her breath was matching his movements.

Every long stroke prodded her closer to that height he'd helped her find before. With the fifth one she gasped, trembling on that exquisite precipice. With the sixth, she shattered.

Jeremy grit his jaw, digging his fingers into the mattress as Tracy shuddered, her muscles tugging at him as she went over the edge, calling him to follow. When she sighed, her grip on his back turning into soft strokes, he sat back enough to see her face, keeping himself buried inside her.

"Cheater," he said, trying to infuse the word with humor despite the need pounding through him, demanding he find his own release.

A surprised chuckle popped her lips open. She was so beautiful, hair tousled, cheeks pinkened, satisfaction clear in every line of her face, the unselfconscious sprawl of her torso.

"Maybe we should pick a different number," Jeremy mused with false calm. "Fifteen seems like too much…" *Damn straight*, his dick agreed.

Tracy's eyes widened warily.

"Thirteen?" Jeremy suggested, still teasing. But her muscles tightened around him again at the thought, a little moan escaping her.

He paused to take a deep breath, then another. Focused on kissing her to give himself another moment to gather the shreds of his control. By the time he braced above her again, she was clutching him in pure anticipation.

"Wait for me this time," he whispered. But instead of pulling out and starting over, he withdrew just barely, then sank deep again. He hadn't tried it this way before, but the idea had to be about the same. That or he would slowly commit suicide, stroke by stroke.

After twelve of the pulsing movements deep inside her, Jeremy gave in to the longer one they both wanted. They groaned in unison.

Buried in her again, he fought every instinct in order to stick to the plan: Eleven short, two long. Ten short, three long.

By the time he hit eight and five, Tracy's teeth had sunk into his shoulder, even the smaller movements making her whimper with need. The promise of having her come apart in his arms again nearly tempted him to give in. But this way should be even better for her than before. Her little panting sighs at the seven short strokes strengthened his resolve. A low moan accompanied each of the six long.

Halfway there. He was too far gone to say it out loud. Every bit of his control was on maintaining the even pace. Six short, seven long.

Five short, eight long.

He faltered, forcing air in through gritted teeth as Tracy squeezed him closer. A hand traveled down his back, gripping his ass as if offering permission to give them what they both wanted *now.*

But Jeremy was a stubborn bastard. Catching his earlier pace, he found his spot. Just four short, then nine blessedly long, full strokes. Tracy's hips met him for each one, as eager as he was.

At eleven long, she was quivering beneath him, fighting to hold herself back, to stay with him. With the last short one, Jeremy dropped a kiss above her ear. "Now," he groaned, burying his face in her hair as he drove into her.

She held on for the first few strokes, her body trembling in protest. But by five she let him take her over the edge again. His hips kept pumping as she shuddered and clenched around him once more, moaning her pleasure. Her muscles milked him with every stroke as he finally lost count, surrendering to release.

Chapter Seventeen

JEREMY NUZZLED HER TEMPLE, murmured, "Be right back," then rolled away and off the bed to disappear into the bathroom. Tracy let herself stare up at the ceiling, her body still tingling from that last orgasm. With a satisfied sigh, she slipped under the covers.

The water in the bathroom shut off, and she tossed the comforter aside, holding the sheet close as she pulled her knees up. Jeremy came out, entirely unconcerned with his nudity, so she didn't stop herself from running her eyes over his body. She'd barely gotten to explore it, not that she was complaining about what they *had* done. The question was, what happened now?

He lowered to the edge of the bed, a hand landing on her knee. "Regrets?"

Tracy shook her head and forced her shoulders to drop. "You?"

Indulgent humor touched his eyes, the corners of his lips. He brushed her hair back, cupping her head, and leaned in for a soft kiss. "So what are you thinking?" he asked, letting his fingers play with the tangled mess of her hair, trace over the curve of her ear. "Cuddling or lunch?"

She laughed, trailing her fingers up his chest. He caught her hand, holding it over his heartbeat.

"You don't have to stay if you don't want to," Tracy pointed out. They were both adults, and sex didn't have to mean anything more. She didn't want him sticking around out of some misplaced sense of courtesy.

"Oh, I see." His hand dropped from her hair, skimming from her shoulder back down to her knees. "Got what you wanted and now you're getting rid of me."

She mirrored his smile. "Exactly."

They settled on a compromise: ordering in lunch and making space for the shelf he'd built her as they waited. They also compromised on attire, Jeremy leaving off his shirt so Tracy would wear it. Despite his teasing protests, she'd slipped on panties as well. But it was nice, being surrounded by his slightly spicy scent as she cleared out the corner.

More than once she'd straightened from moving a box to catch Jeremy staring at her ass. She would have called him out on it, but some part of her liked that he still found her attractive—that his interest hadn't waned the second he got what he'd been after since the beginning. Besides, she liked watching the play of his muscles as he helped, so saying something would have just made her a hypocrite.

A knock signaled the arrival of their lunch, and Tracy dropped her stack of preview booklets onto the nearest box.

"Tracy?" Jeremy said as she moved to the door. "Pants," he added when she glanced at him, failing to hide his smile.

Right. She might not get fully dressed every day just to sit down to write, but unlike now, she was usually presentable enough to open the door. Her cheeks heated and she crossed her arms. Jeremy just watched her, humor dancing in his eyes, until the knock came again.

"I'm going to go get dressed," Tracy announced, picking her way back to the bedroom.

"Shame," he murmured, heading toward the door.

"Ask you something?" Jeremy said once they'd made a dent in the Chinese food.

Tracy's bare legs lay tangled with his between them on the couch. She'd switched out his tee shirt for a loose sleeveless top, a pink bra peeking through distractingly from underneath, and pulled her skirt back on.

"Sure." She stretched against the arm of the couch, completely unaware of how the movement showcased her breasts.

She'd looked so sexy perched on the back, bent over his arm as her sighs egged him on. Given the chance, he'd pleasure her on every surface in her apartment. And his.

But moments like this in between, relaxing together, were nearly as enticing.

"Why'd you wait?" he asked. She'd commented on social expectations, on reader assumptions. But the decision must have mattered to her in a more personal way.

Her exhale sounded heavy.

Jeremy skimmed his knuckles up her leg. "I don't mean to pry."

"No, it's—" Her small frown creased between her eyebrows. "I've never really put it into words, I guess."

She drew her legs back from his touch, tucking them under her instead. He bent his, too, curling his bare toes into the plush area rug.

"I started reading romance pretty young, so when it came to fooling around or sex, I always knew it was supposed to feel good." She shook her head impatiently. "It sounds trite, I know. But for many girls, women, that's a radical statement. If it didn't feel good, I didn't do it for the sake of keeping some boy happy. People have the most awful first time stories—not everyone, of course, but so many women especially. I guess, even when I was younger I didn't want to be the object some guy humped for his pleasure."

Jeremy nodded, setting aside the carton of fried rice he still held. Unfortunately, it wasn't surprising that so many girls still weren't taught their pleasure mattered too.

"As I got older, guys I went out with grew impatient. They knew I didn't object to sex in general, so why not sex with them? I wasn't going to say it was because their clumsy rushing to the 'end game' wasn't, well, sexy." Her breath huffed out at the memories, but then her eyes met his clearly. "Telling a guy he isn't any good…"

She didn't need to finish the thought. He knew how that one felt first-hand.

"The better relationships I had went slower, ended for other reasons. I tried the casual route, going home with someone I met at a bar." Tracy shrugged, lips twisting in a rueful smile, and stabbed absently at the remaining orange chicken in her hands. "Most often it was still… Disappointing. I was more turned on by the things I wrote than the way they fumbled, pawing at me. I hated feeling like I could be replaced by any willing orifice. And it definitely wasn't going to be something I tolerated just to get it over with, as if not having had sex somehow made me less of a person all that time than I am now."

"Definitely not," Jeremy said, not that she needed his confirmation.

Still she shot him a little smile. "Eventually, assumptions were made about my experience, and I got into my head. So even if I did enjoy fooling around, the pressure of what would come next, what was expected of me, got in the way." One shoulder lifted and dropped.

It made sense. When he'd rushed her, it had been like stomping on the brakes while tossing the engine out of the car.

Jeremy'd brought the topic up, but what could he say now? He understood a little more, which was what he'd wanted. There was something extraordinary about the steel core that had let her live according to her convictions, knowing she deserved better despite all the external pressure she must have felt.

"Hope I was worth the wait," he finally said. Like a complete and utter moron.

It had to be a joke, despite the careful way Jeremy continued to watch her. After all that, he couldn't possibly doubt he'd left her fully satisfied.

"Practice makes perfect," Tracy teased in response, setting down the leftover food she'd fiddled with as she talked.

"Angling for another round?" he asked, lips tugging up though that odd undercurrent lingered.

A little shiver worked through her insides at the reminder of round one. And two and three. "You got it from a book, didn't you?" Tracy asked about his counting method. Curiosity had been niggling the back of her mind, even if she'd been too distracted at the time.

He knew exactly what she meant, a thread of self-satisfaction transforming his smile. "Yours aren't the only romances I've read," he admitted. "Jealous?" he added, standing to walk over to the bookshelf that still waited awkwardly angled in front of her door. His muscles bunched as he lifted it, sending a fresh lick of warmth through her.

"Good to have some new inspiration," she quipped, also getting up to move a bag of pins out of his way. "It really is beautiful," she said when he'd settled the shelf in its new spot.

"Thanks." His palm lingered on the wood, as if reluctant to part ways. With a deep breath, he patted it and tucked his hands into his pockets. "Not as beautiful as you," he redirected, that slightly self-deprecating smile of his reappearing.

"So corny," she murmured, stepping closer to trail a fingertip along the grooves in the top surface that mimicked book pages.

"I'll try to stop." The words were soft, almost sad. His throat worked as he swallowed, watching her caress his gift.

Tracy raised her hand to his jaw, coming close enough that his jeans brushed her legs. "Jeremy, no," she said equally quietly, staring into the shadowed depths of his eyes. "I'm sorry, I was teasing."

He brushed his knuckles down her cheek then tucked his face into her neck, pulling her in for a hug.

Tracy curled her fingers in his hair, wrapping her other arm around his torso. "Want to talk about it?" she asked against his skin.

His silence answered for him, his chest rising and falling with his breath. It was like she'd accidentally hit on something raw deep within him, the wound that still made him worry he wasn't good enough—and not just in bed. Sure, Tracy only knew part of the story, but resentment burned through her at his ex-wife's cruelty.

"I just…" Jeremy started eventually. "I don't want to do anything to ruin this." His embrace eased, and he would have backed away if Tracy's arms hadn't kept him within reach. "Like assuming there is a *this* now."

Because the last time he had, she'd snapped at him for wanting Taralynn. For not seeing her, even though she'd kept anything real hidden, too worried about not measuring up. Just like he still was. They were such a perfect mess of insecurities.

"I have an idea," she said, letting her hands slip to his chest. "How about you be you, and I be me, and we'll just see how things go when we're not trying to live up to assumptions of what the other person wants?" Easier said than done, but they could at least try, couldn't they?

Jeremy hesitated then sighed, the tension seeping away as something calmer settled within him. His hands skimmed up her ribs, closing the slight distance between their bodies. "It's almost like you're an expert on how a healthy relationship should go," he said, lips slanting into his adorable crooked smile.

Tracy laughed. That was one way of looking at the stories she wrote. "Almost. The real-life version might look a little different."

He turned away to glance around the disaster zone her living room had become, with stacks from this corner shifted wherever they could land for now and takeout containers still littering her coffee table. When he turned back to her, something heated yet hopeful filtered in under the humor. "Looks pretty great to me."

Tracy shook her head at the line, giving in to her grin as she rose up for a kiss. "Yeah," she murmured against his lips. "Me too."

Acknowledgments

I hope those below already know how grateful I am, but I'd still like to shine a quick spotlight on:

Rachel, the first person who heard this story idea and somehow stayed enthusiastic about it all this time;

Joanne, Jami, and Jennifer (the *J*s were a coincidence!), who bravely dove into the rough draft of a very important set of scenes;

My Patrons, who believe in my writing and patiently stood by me as I slogged my way through the first draft;

All the friends who keep me (relatively) sane;

And the family members who love me through everything: Words aren't enough.

Love contemporary romances?
Read on for an excerpt from:

Fragments That Fit

Chapter One

Son of a—

Not that Shoshi should have been surprised, really. Of *course* on the day she'd been running late for work, and there'd been no parking at the Chestnut Hill stop—so she'd had to shell out twenty bucks to park in the city—her car would die. And her ancient cell phone's battery would, too.

Shoshi dropped the useless thing in her purse and trudged toward the only place that looked open, which was—of course—a bar. Not exactly the best place to find herself stranded alone after midnight.

But it was her best hope for a phone, and to avoid freezing to death in the middle of the street.

Shoshi pulled the door open and stepped into the darkened room, stamping her boots free of snow on the waiting mat. A few patrons glanced her way, but otherwise no one seemed to pay her any attention, thank G-d.

She walked over to the bar and tugged off her gloves. When the bartender looked up, she shot him a tight smile, her cheeks still tingling from the change in temperature. He frowned, sizing her up, but made his way over.

"Hi," she exhaled when he reached her.

"What can I get you?" he asked in a weary monotone.

Could she ask for the phone without ordering something? Best-case scenario, his eyes would shoot daggers her way the entire time she was here. What was the cheapest drink she could stomach nursing while she waited for help? "Just half a pint of whatever cider you have on tap."

He nodded, tossing a cardboard coaster onto the bar.

"Wait," she added as he started moving away. "Listen, I'm really sorry, but my cell's dead and my car won't start. Is there a phone here I could use?"

He stared at her for a few pounding heartbeats then turned to pick up a handset. Shoshi sighed, pushing her hair back from her face and trying to smooth down the grease-coated frizz before he turned back around. She aimed for a grateful smile when he handed her the phone. "Thank you."

He didn't respond.

Nat's voicemail greeted Shoshi's first attempt to rouse her potential savior from sleep. She hung up and hit redial. The bartender set her cider down before shifting toward a man who came up to trade his empty glass for a fresh drink. Shoshi angled her body away.

Right before the rings clicked off onto voicemail for a third time, a groggy voice muttered, "Who's this?"

Shoshi stifled the pang of guilt. "Nat, I'm so sorry, but it's Shoshana." She waited, but there was only silence. "You there?"

"What's wrong?" It wasn't even really a question.

"My car's dead. I need a tow, and I'd call triple A or someone, but you know they take forever at night, and I have this super important interview tomorrow that I'm woefully underqualified for, so not sleeping definitely wouldn't help, and—"

Shoshi bit back the flow of words. "I'll make it up to you," she promised.

"Yeah, yeah. Where are you?"

A wave of relief eased the tension thrumming through her. "Dalton and Scotia." She glanced around for the name of the bar. "At the Roaring Serpent."

"Got it," Nat said and unceremoniously hung up.

Shoshi set the phone on the edge of the bar and took a deep breath, letting it out slowly before sipping the cider. It wasn't awful. She unzipped her jacket a little, settling in for the wait. It would take Nat at least twenty minutes to get here, but that still meant Shoshi would make it home in about an hour and a half. Hopefully. Other than the fact that her car being out of commission meant she had no way to get to her interview tomorrow, it was all fine. She could handle it.

When the bartender came by to pick up the handset, the man she'd noticed earlier moved closer, looking her up and down. Shoshi shot him a polite half-smile and refocused on her cider.

"Rough night?" The man's deep, sleek voice interrupted her scrutiny of the stream of bubbles in her glass. His self-assured smirk and a disquieting glint in his eyes killed any remaining interest she might have had in being social.

"I'm fine," Shoshi brushed off.

His eyes trained on the region of her chest, focusing on the vee of skin exposed between the edges of her coat. "If you're worried about getting to bed, my place is only a short walk away."

"That's charming." Her head shook unevenly. *Un-friggin'-believable.* "Because what I need to top off this crappy, crappy day are the drunk advances of someone with nothing better to do than hang out alone in a bar in the middle of a Tuesday night, who couldn't even be bothered to ask my name before suggesting we sleep together. Not that that basic human courtesy would have changed anything. But lucky me, your place is nearby."

Unfazed, he raised his tumbler to his lips and sipped the dark liquid, gaze trained on her. "I didn't say anything about sleep."

Shoshi rolled her eyes, turning away once again. A long sip of her cider did little to clear the bad taste of the brief exchange.

"And your name is Shoshana," the man added.

Her head snapped toward him. *How…?*

Then her brain caught up. "Eavesdropping. You're just full of impressive traits, aren't you. Haven't you ever heard of manners? I mean really, do these half-assed lines ever even work?"

One of his eyebrows crooked, emphasizing his pale eyes. Eyes that were once again examining her, lingering over the messy mass of her hair, the collar of her Wendy's uniform, the un-manicured hand resting on the bar. His head turned slightly, indicating toward the room behind him.

Shoshi glanced in the same direction. There were no other women in the bar, at least none that she could see.

"Slow night," he said, as if his gesture needed further explanation. She was nothing more than a last resort.

Sure, she was no knockout even on her best day. After a nine-hour shift that left her smelling like grease—even though she'd mostly been on register tonight—and months subsisting on fast food meals, *sexy* would be the last way to describe her.

Meanwhile, this man with his square jaw, chiseled cheeks, and impossibly symmetrical dark features juxtaposing his light skin—not to mention broad shoulders and fit build beneath a nice, if slightly rumpled, suit—would be appreciated by any straight woman with a pulse. Until he started speaking, anyway.

But that really wasn't the point. "Shocking how the women of Boston have something better to do than wait around to service you, isn't it?" Shoshi asked deadpan.

The corner of his lips quirked up, and his eyes ran over her body again, assessing rather than appreciating.

One of them was saved from further comment by the blinking lights of a tow truck pulling up outside. Shoshi dug into her purse for her last ten-dollar bill and set it by her unfinished drink. "Thanks for all your help," she called to the bartender, who'd stayed strategically away from the two of them, before heading outside.

All she had to do was make it to her place, and then she could officially put this night behind her. At least until she had to figure out how to get to her interview. And how to make this up to Nat. And how to cover the bill for her car repairs.

Yeah. Everything was totally under control.

Chapter Two

"YOU'RE NOT WHAT I'M LOOKING FOR," Luc Davin said without even looking up when a secretary showed Shoshi into his office the next morning.

She froze half a step inside the door. "I don't understand," she admitted after a touch too long.

When the regional vice president of one of the biggest venture capital firms in Boston did look up, recognition momentarily dropped Shoshi's jaw. She snapped it closed. "Oh. Now I do."

Davin's eyebrows jerked upward, and his eyes trailed over her body for the umpteenth time in twelve hours. He was really going to deny her a job because she'd turned down his coarse come-on? She'd wasted money on cab fare for this!

His gaze dropped to the tablet he held before coming back to her. "Shana Glass." He paused. "You applied under a fake name?"

"It's the name I use professionally." Neutral enough not to sound "ethnic" and a perfectly reasonable shortening of Shoshana. "I'm sure your birth certificate says *Luc* on it, right?"

He let the tablet displaying what had to be her résumé drift down onto the lacquered desk. "As I said, you aren't right for this position." He turned to the computer angled toward him. The dismissal was unmistakable.

"Then why ask me in for an interview?" Shoshi challenged, stepping a bit further into the room. Her fingers dug into the portfolio she held so she wouldn't fiddle nervously with the charm around her neck. This was the first interview she'd gotten in months of applying to positions that would actually use her master's degree in finance. She couldn't afford to simply walk away.

He sighed, then leaned back in his chair. Unlike last night, his suit was crisp, the slate tie carefully knotted. "HR handles pre-screenings for positions. Someone must have made a mistake. How was it you put it? You're *woefully underqualified.*"

So there wasn't going to be even a hint of professionalism. Then again, with his reputation, Luc Davin could do whatever the hell he wanted. His methodical—though now she suspected ruthless—rise to regional VP of Griffith & Moore was incomparable. *Admirable*, she would have said before meeting him. He must not have been as drunk as she'd thought if he could quote her words back at her so easily. Was there any way to salvage this?

"Look, Mr. Davin, despite my private comment to a friend last night and completely natural pre-interview nerves, I can assure you, I am more than capable enough to be your next finance director." *Liar.* This job was way out of her league. It was also her only option, one she couldn't let slip away, even if someone's mistake was the only reason she stood there now. "I may not have as many years of experience as some of your other candidates, but I am determined, efficient, and adaptive.

If we could both agree to move on past last night's unfortunate—"

"Enough."

Shoshi's lips clamped shut. The lascivious drinker from the night before had nothing in common with the calculating, astute, and obviously capable man in front of her now. A man who saw right through her practiced bravado.

"We both know you were reaching when you applied for this job. Director of finance? With four months at Keres Financial as your most relevant experience? Doesn't exactly recommend you."

At least she'd anticipated that being brought up. "I'm sure you can understand attributing that situation to me is about as reasonable as blaming your junior associates for any of your hypothetical misconduct."

"Ignorance isn't a particularly desirable attribute in an employee. No one in their right mind would hire you for a position like this." He glanced at the tablet again. "Though I see you left Wendy's off your résumé."

The derision in his expression notched her chin up a fraction. Heat filled her cheeks, and malicious enjoyment touched his eyes. There was no question he was relishing dressing her down after the night before, even if he was right—on paper, this job was so far out of her reach. She'd only applied out of a growing desperation to escape the fast food world.

"It didn't seem relevant," Shoshi managed in response to his dig.

"And even if you *were* otherwise qualified," he continued, "the way you comported yourself last night proves you're not ready for a position that would require you to represent a company such as ours with all manner of professionals from all over the world."

"And what about your behavior last night?" she asked, her tone remaining remarkably even. "How well did that reflect on this company?"

His expression didn't change.

She held his sharp gaze a moment longer in the resulting silence. "Thanks for your time and consideration," she said on autopilot before heading out the door.

Shoshi kept it together until she made it out of the firm's office space and ducked into the hallway bathroom, which was thankfully single-occupancy. She locked the door and leaned against it, blowing her breath out in a steady stream as her eyes prickled. When that didn't help, she pounded her fist gently against the door, her other hand fingering the hamsa charm her dad had given her for her Bat Mitzvah. She'd worn it for luck and courage, a reminder of the encouragement he would have offered had he known about the interview. It hadn't been enough. Because *she* wasn't enough. None of this was supposed to be this hard.

Shoshi'd had a plan. Her father's life insurance money had mostly been spent on covering his healthcare bills, so freshman year of college, she'd sold the house. That money had run out midway through her senior year, but loans and part-time work had seen her through her master's. Landing the job at Keres Financial was supposed to mean a stable future, even if it was a commission-based position. That was when she'd left her education off her résumé and picked up some shifts at Wendy's.

It was only supposed to be temporary, a way to survive while she proved herself. An offer from Keres had been everyone's dream. Until it turned out the firm's executives had engaged in some extremely shady—read: illegal—practices. Not that anyone else at the company had been aware, much less Shoshi, who'd only been there a few months when everything came to light. But she also hadn't been there long enough to establish her own reputation, and now no one wanted to hire her.

Shoshi had done everything "right," but so what? She was still stuck two years later, balancing her hours at Wendy's and her "side job" at Dunkin' Donuts while sending her résumé to every moderately relevant listing she could find.

She wasn't alone in the endless job hunt, of course. Plenty of recent graduates struggled to find positions related to their field of study, relying on their parents or moving home.

Shoshi had neither.

Just a worthless degree, a mountain of debt, and two dead-end jobs. At least she could eat half her meals at work, though G-d only knew what the repercussions for *that* would be down the line.

Not that it mattered now. Since coming here had turned out to be a waste of time, she had to get out of this bathroom and back to Riverside so she could call a cab, get to the mechanic's, and hopefully get her car before she had to head to work. Lingering disinfectant coated the inside of her nose, like the building itself was eager to wipe any trace of her from the premises, but Shoshi was happy to oblige. She splashed some water on her cheeks then ran her fingers over her hair to catch the frizz no styling product could entirely control, even if she could have afforded one. With a fresh coat of lip balm slathered over her lips, she tugged on her coat and picked up the faux-leather portfolio Bentley had given them all right before graduation. As if the thin folder would help them land jobs.

The hallway was silent, Griffith & Moore's secretary perfectly centered behind their glass doors. Shoshi turned and headed to the bank of elevators. Luc Davin may be one of the most successful men in Boston's financial world, but there was no way she could have worked with him, not after her brief but all too informative glimpse into his personality.

This was for the best, she told herself as the elevator descended. It had to be.

Luc tapped the screen and dragged Shoshana Glass's application file into the Rejected folder. He'd have to have a talk with whoever had passed her through to this interview. He would have thought it was a poor excuse for a prank, if she hadn't actually shown up with that barely buried disgust in her eyes.

Not that anyone in the company would prank Luc Davin. No, someone had made a stupid or thoughtless mistake and wasted his time.

Shoshana Glass was inexperienced, with a degree whose shine had quickly worn off and an aura of desperation. She might have hidden it better today than the night before, but it was there. Along with a seething disdain for him, and just enough of a backbone to make her interesting.

Keep Reading:

fragments.ariaglazki.com

About Aria

Aria Glazki's first kiss technically came from a bear cub. Though no fairytale transformation followed, she still believes magic can happen when the right people come together—if they don't get in their own way, that is. So now Aria writes heartfelt romances about relatable people overcoming real-world obstacles to build love that lasts.

Aria Glazki

Relatable People — Remarkable Love

www.AriaGlazki.com